MAPMAKER

Praise for *Mapmaker*

"[Bomback and Craze's] clever and resourceful heroine . . . [fuses] Mia Thermopolis with Jason Bourne . . . Taut and techy . . . Fair warning: after finishing *Mapmaker*, you might find yourself looking over your shoulder or leaving that smartphone at home for a few days."

—*The Christian Science Monitor*

"Haunting and compelling—Tanya repeatedly thinks she is successfully hiding only to discover that there is really no such thing as off the grid . . . Tech-inspired readers will love the idea of MapOut, and they'll appreciate the point that the impact of new technology depends on who's wielding it."

—*The Bulletin of the Center for Children's Books*

"Bomback and Craze show us the world through the eyes of a young woman whose unique and remarkable gift is also a terrible burden. *Mapmaker* expertly brings the paranoid thriller into the age of surveillance, and the result is both moving and chilling."   —**D.B. Weiss, co-creator, writer, and producer of *Game of Thrones***

"*Mapmaker* is a must-read thriller, with a courageous and intelligent heroine, a compelling mystery, and an ending that will leave you hungry for more. Fast-paced, smart, and dangerous—I couldn't put it down!"   —**Jennifer A. Nielsen, *New York Times* bestselling author of *The False Prince***

"*Mapmaker* is the terrifying lovechild of swashbuckling exploration and ruthless human surveillance. You'll want to have your atlas handy, your cyber smokescreen installed and your wits about you for this one."
—**Elizabeth Kiem, author of *Dancer, Daughter, Traitor, Spy***

"Bomback and Craze whip up a suspense-laden, modern mystery that pulls on the current obsession with technology, mapping, and tracking people's locations—and how innocently supplied data can be turned to a darker purpose."
—*Booklist*

"Fans of Michelle Gagnon's *Don't Turn Around* will enjoy this work for its exploration of the dangers of a technology-connected world . . . [An] action-packed, plot-centric thriller."
—*School Library Journal*

"Fast paced and well executed, this mystery thriller will have readers devouring page after page . . . A deep and dark look at technology and where it might be headed, with a commentary on how disappearing in our modern world is far more difficult than it once was."
—*VOYA*

"A thriller that offers a frightening glimpse into how technology can be abused . . . Thought-provoking."
—*Publishers Weekly*

"[Readers will] identify with Tanya's inability to hide in our high-tech world."
—*Kirkus Reviews*

MAPMAKER

Mark Bomback
Galaxy Craze

Published in the United States by Soho Teen
an imprint of
Soho Press, Inc.
853 Broadway
New York, NY 10003

Library of Congress Cataloging-in-Publication Data
Bomback, Mark.
Mapmaker / Mark Bomback, Galaxy Craze.

ISBN 978-1-61695-633-2
eISBN 978-1-61695-350-8

1. Mystery and detective stories. 2. Cartography—Fiction. 3. Maps—Fiction. 4.
Secrets—Fiction. I. Craze, Galaxy. II. Title.
PZ7.1.B66 Map 2015   [Fic]—dc23   2014030130

Interior design by Janine Agro, Soho Press, Inc.

Printed in the United States of America

10 9 8 7 6 5 4 3 2 1

For Tema, Miles, Caroline, Annie and Phoebe. My true north.
—Mark

For Anna Mirabai Lytton,
a young writer whose creativity is now light upon the water.
—Galaxy

MAPMAKER

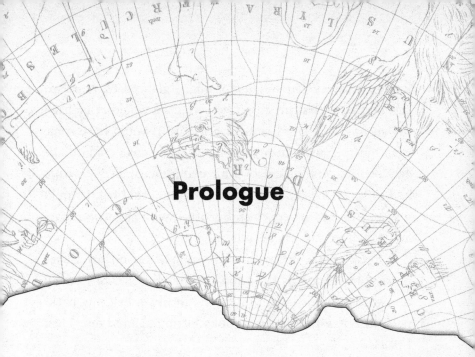

Prologue

Dad's home.

That was my first thought when I saw the footprints in the snow, leading to the front door of our house. The tracks were large, a man's shoe size, and as I looked closer I saw the unmistakable zigzag imprint of his boots. He must have come home early, walking along the bike trail from MapOut. Maybe his office closed early because of the forecast; the blizzard would only get worse.

Our house was white with black shutters and two red-brick chimneys on either side. It reminded me of a guard dog: leaded-glass bedroom windows for eyes; the two chimneys for ears; the black front door, the nose. I'd lived here my whole life. The house was the one constant, the one thing that had remained while so much else had changed. The house was the one place I felt safe. The house *was* my guard dog.

The excitement of Dad's being home early was something I hadn't felt in a long time, like waking up at dawn and knowing it was Christmas morning. I glanced over toward the garage. Beth's car wasn't here yet; she wouldn't be back for an hour or two. I smiled. Dad and I would have some time together without my stepmom. Maybe we could make extra-strong hot chocolate with plain cocoa, maple syrup, and milk. If he was working (I knew he would be), I would just curl up on the couch in his office with the woodstove, and watch the cinders burn.

I followed the footsteps. The snowflakes on my lashes blurred my vision as I ran toward the house. *Dad's home*: the words sounded again in my mind like a bell, my back-pack heavy with a laptop, books hitting against me. Then I paused.

I did something I hadn't allowed myself do since I was little. I stepped in one of his tracks in the snow, my boot print covering his.

Staring down at the footsteps, I tried to catch my breath. Something was wrong. I slipped as I scrambled toward the front porch. My knee cracked against the edge of the first wooden step. Pain shot through my body as I pushed myself up; my fingers burned red from the cold. I reached for the handle of the front door—and stopped cold at my reflection in the window.

Of course these weren't my father's footprints. My father was dead.

What was wrong with me? How could I have let myself pre-tend he was alive, even for a second? I took a step back, away from the house. I followed the length of my own footsteps, now trying to calculate how many steps and for how long I'd deluded myself. Twenty seconds at the most? The feeling I'd had was so hopeful, so real.

Turning back to the black shutters, the windows as dark as lake water, I felt a fear I could barely name. For the first time in my life, I was afraid of my own mind. My mother died when I was ten—and never, not once, not even in my dreams, had I ever forgotten. My mother's death was like a badge I wore, forever pinned to my chest.

I blinked. The reality of my life fell back into focus: the loneliness inside that house, the empty rooms behind the windows, the dark glass reflecting the falling snow, the evergreen branches closing in like a gate. The heat would be set low for the workday, my father's office deserted and still—no fire in the small woodstove, no one sitting at his desk, no books opened to the previous night's page. The large upstairs bedroom my mother and father once shared: abandoned. Even my stepmother wouldn't sleep there alone. After my father's death, Beth moved into the tiny guest room my mother had painted her favorite shade of pale blue.

There was a zigzag pattern in the snow. That *was* the print on his soles. Those were his favorite boots. He had bought them in Vermont in grad school and still wore them every winter. But I was too old for this, too smart to let myself ever be fooled by signs or miracles or look-alikes. The boots must have belonged to the mailman, the furnace repairman, a college kid working for Greenpeace. That this person wore the same brand was just a cruel coincidence.

I took a step backward, then another and another, moving away from the house.

Fear was a cold feeling. This was a safe town. We hardly

ever locked our house or car. Sometimes police were called for an overly noisy frat party or a lost dog wandering the streets, but that was it. I told myself this as I hurried up the slope to the sidewalk.

The afternoon was growing dim, the white sky turning grey. The lights of the passing cars glowed through the snow-flakes.

I stood on the roadside, in what I assumed was the safety of being visible to the slow-moving cars. From the top of the slope, I kept my eyes on the vanishing trail. I saw the route now: he had come from the woods and walked to our front door before returning around the side of our house across the yard to the shed—where the trail ended.

There was an arch-pattern that would have only resulted from the door being opened. Meaning someone was hiding inside the shed. But why?

There was nothing that a thief would want. The shed was full of my father's old encyclopedias, a large wooden desk made from two-by-fours, and a wooden chair. He used to work there in the spring and summer. The windows looked out to the narrow creek, the maple trees.

My dad never brought his computer into the shed, just his books and a thermos of tea. He scoured rare travel diaries and out-of-print history texts, studied landscape and waterways and topography. He read about nomads, exotic expeditions, import and export shipping. He told me that the best way to learn how people think is through the routes they take. The art of mapmaking was not just in precision and measurements, but in the ways we negotiate the climate and texture of the land around us.

There was only one thing of any value inside: Between the two windows on the wide-plank wooden boards hung a framed lithograph of the Piri Reis map.

Like a favorite painting or poem or song, Dad had a favorite map. The original was drawn in 1513, on gazelle-skin parchment. Its claim to fame over six centuries was its incredible accuracy. Piri Reis, a navigator—a bit of a wild man, according to my father—rendered it long before most cartographers began to account for the curvature of the earth. Yet it matched perfectly with modern satellite imagery from a geosynchronous orbit, 25,000 miles up.

Like Piri Reis, my father passionately believed that in order to map, one had to explore the terrain firsthand. Dad understood the Earth, too, in all its curves and secrets. He never sent assistants with high-tech computers to do the job for him. Wherever and whenever he traveled for work, he only took a roller of measuring tape, food, a supply of water, and sun block. I remember his partner snickering behind his back when he'd say for the hundredth time: *"I map the land with my own eyes."*

It was the motto he lived by. The motto he died by.

My mother had found the print in an antique shop in Boston. It was expensive for her at the time; Dad had just started MapOut with his best friend and my godfather, and he had put most of our family's savings into the business. I remember standing beside her in the shop as she examined it for what seemed like hours. I remember tugging at her hand, impatient to leave a place that smelled of dust and old books. She told the man she would have to think about it, and we left the shop without it. She'd gone back without telling either my dad or me.

I crouched low, moving quickly from my spot behind the maple to get a closer look at the shed. Then I dropped down on my hands and knees in the snow, crawling through the underbrush of hedgerows. I was fifty feet away—fifty-one at most—but the falling snow and the darkening sky blurred the edges of anything visible.

Dusk, my father used to warn, was the most dangerous light.

Never once had I been anxious for Beth to come home. Not until this moment. I pulled my phone from my pocket to call her or the police. But the lit screen wouldn't respond to my touch. In frustration, I punched my passcode harder, again and again. Nothing. The phone had frozen in the cold. I stared as snowflakes melted on it.

The police station was under a mile away: 1,460 yards from doorstep to doorstep. Running, I could make it there in less than fifteen minutes. But I'd made that calculation on a day without snow. Besides, I knew I would never leave. I would wait. This was my house. If I wanted to feel safe again, to sleep tonight, I needed to know that whoever was in the shed was gone.

I sat on my backpack. I hugged my knees close to my chest, pulling my coat sleeves around my numb fingers, making myself as small as possible.

I'm not sure how long I sat there. The grey afternoon sky turned charcoal. I was so cold I lost feeling in my hands and toes.

Finally a sound came from the shed: wood hitting wood. The door opened, only an inch or two, slowly pushing against the weight of the snow. I squinted. The air was like smoke now, thick and almost impenetrable. The houses and trees had lost all definition; they were silhouettes.

I saw the shape of a man in the doorway, looking from left to right. I couldn't make out his features. He wore a hat, a heavy coat. I squinted, desperate to determine his height or build, but he was only a dark shadow. I assumed he would head back the way of the bike path but he didn't. He stopped and placed his hands in his coat pocket, looking up at the windows of our house. He stood there for only a second or two, but I was struck by his confidence. The casual arrogance of the gesture. Then he turned quickly down the slope, leaping across the narrowest part of the creek. Clearly, he knew this property well.

And now he was gone.

I stood, brushing the snow off. I couldn't go inside the house; I couldn't be alone. I'd waited all this time only to see a shadow. I reached for my backpack, soaked from the snow, and walked quickly down Lincoln Road toward the center of town.

As I paused for the streetlight to change, I thought about the way the figure had put his hands in his coat pockets, the way he'd turned to our house. There was something so familiar about his attitude, the tilt of his head, his gait. I stared at the blinking streetlight, with a strange, haunted feeling inside.

I was sure I knew him. But at the same time I had no clue who he was.

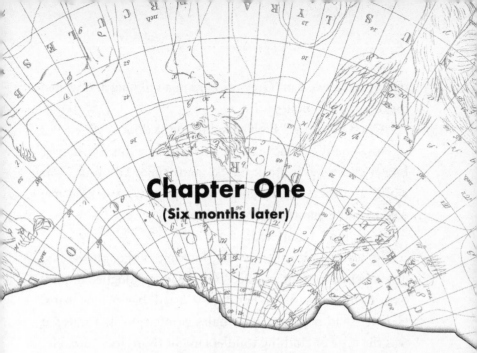

Chapter One
(Six months later)

From the corner of my eye I saw Beth's shadow cross the floor.

Really? I groaned to myself.

She had promised she would sleep in. School was out for summer; she wouldn't be back in the kindergarten classroom until after Labor Day. The last thing I wanted this morning was a conversation with Beth. I searched my pockets for my phone. I'd already put it in my backpack. Besides, it was too early to fake-text like I normally did.

Outside the kitchen window everything was green and gold, except for the river, which ran a glittering dark blue. The birds flitted from the porch roof to the small wooden birdhouse. Back and forth, back and forth, again and again. They were so nervous. Maybe they thought that they were stealing Beth's stash of seeds. Beth's stash wouldn't run out if every bird in New England showed up.

The kitchen floor felt cold against my bare feet, and I stared at the teakettle. The flame under it burned blue and red. I placed two Earl Grey tea bags in a tall mug and waited for the water to boil.

"Good morning," Beth called from the doorway.

How could she move so quietly through this old house? Like a ghost, never creaking. So many times I'd think I was alone, and there she'd appear in a doorway, watching me. And then the questions would come . . .

"Morning," I muttered.

She walked into the kitchen, looking as though she had just stepped out of a 1985 L.L.Bean catalogue, a pink oxford shirt tucked into her high-waisted, baggy blue jeans. Her belt had a pattern of whales printed on it. I guess it was the type of clothing toddlers might think was cute. Her thick brown hair was pulled back into a high ponytail. She even had a rope bracelet—a gift from one of her kindergarten students.

I forced a smile, which felt more like a grimace. I knew she only had good intentions. She wanted to be here for me on my first day of "work," like a mother or father would have been, like mine should have been. After all, "work" was a paid internship at my dad's company, MapOut, the company he'd devoted the last part of his short life to founding. But it was her summer vacation. Her worry was only irritating.

The kettle whistled. I reached for the handle without thinking, burning the palm of my hand.

"Shit," I snapped, flinching away.

Before I even had a chance to look up, Beth was beside me with an ice pack wrapped in a cloth.

"It's okay," I said, pulling my stinging hand against my chest. I fought back tears of pain and frustration. I glanced up at the clock—7:15—and decided to leave. I'd be an hour and a half early, but that was fine.

"Let me help you," Beth said, laying a hand on my shoulder. Reluctantly I took the ice and held it against my palm. I sat down in the kitchen chair and stared down at nothing. Through the window the birds carried on. They were busy, flying back and forth and back and forth from one bird feeder to the next, feeding their young.

The ice numbed the throbbing. Beth made me my tea with milk and a little honey. She buttered my toast, spread blueberry jam she had canned last summer over it, cut it in half, and placed it all on the table in front of me—complete with a folded cloth napkin.

"Thanks."

She sat down with her cup of coffee. "Hand any better?"

"A little."

"Are you nervous?"

With my unburned hand, I took a sip of tea and shrugged. "Not really."

I'd spent plenty of time at MapOut, so I felt pretty comfortable there. Besides, Harrison Worth, Dad's best friend and MapOut's cofounder, would take care of me. He'd arranged the entire thing. It was all an effort on his part to make up for the fact my grades had plummeted in the six months since Dad had died.

While I resented him for it, I also loved him for it.

I knew I could make more money pouring lattes and cappuccinos at Rao's Coffee. I could have spent the summer with my best friend, Rebs, as a counselor at Camp Norwich. I could have even been a nanny to seven-year-old twin girls in

Provincetown and spent the next few months on the beach. But this would look a lot better on my college applications. That was Harrison's argument, and I couldn't argue back. Dad could never argue with Harrison, either. The man was shrewd and suave and convincing, everything Dad wasn't. It's also why he and my dad made such a great team.

Beth's smile tightened. "You know, you can borrow my car."

"I want to bike," I said, maybe a bit too quickly.

"Your dad would have given anything to be able to take you to work today," Beth said, not even looking at me.

Was she trying to make me cry? I held my breath, forcing myself not to say, *Don't talk about him anymore.* I knew from experience that one way to stop thinking about someone was to stop talking about them. To push forward, to pretend you didn't feel anything. How much longing or regret could someone stand? How many mornings or evenings could I say I wish my mom were here? I wish my dad were here? How much sadness could you let yourself feel? It could swallow you like the sea.

"Tanya . . ." she started to add.

"I better go," I mumbled. I stood up, leaving the tea almost full and the toast untouched. The burn on my hand was still there, pulsing in my palm like a heartbeat. My voice fell onto the ring-stained and scratched wooden tabletop.

Beth nodded, glued to her coffee. "Have a good day," she whispered.

My last image of her that day was her hands wrapped around the mug. Frozen alone at the kitchen table, shoulders hunched forward, brown eyes full of loneliness, shadows of the birds outside playing across her face.

• • •

How would Beth spend the rest of the day? Alone, gardening, cleaning the house? Would she wonder what it was she had said to me that had gone so wrong? Would she remember all the times our conversations had ended up with me slamming my bedroom door? With me reminding her again and again that she was NOT my mother and NEVER would be? When would she give up trying with me? I guess that's what I wanted, and that's what I was trying to make her do: *give up on me.*

Maybe she would go upstairs and lie on my father's side of the bed and sob into the covers. She was forty-four, childless, and now a widow. Beth had wanted a child with my father so badly. They'd spent their marriage trying. They'd visited specialists in Boston. I imagined them climbing up a ladder, a baby waiting at the top. Once it had even worked: Beth had gotten pregnant, and those two months were the happiest I'd ever seen her. Then the heartbeat stopped.

I imagined myself having the courage to go back inside, to give her a hug goodbye. I imagined myself as a different type of girl: someone kinder, less angry. In my mind, when I hugged Beth, I even looked different. In that vision, I smiled. I knew something as simple as that would change her day. It would also change mine.

But the screen door had already slammed.

Halfway across the lawn, I pictured myself from above. I was a speck moving across the grass, a bright point near the river and forest. I rose, and the land below moved outward and outward in my mind until I could see the whole town of Amherst . . . the highest church steeples, the grid of streets, the darker threadlike line of the roads, the thick lane of highway in the distance, the uneven hills surrounding the entire valley.

In my map, I was a pinprick the color of dust, making a wrong turn.

It's so hard to make the easiest change. As I moved farther and farther away from the house, I could see myself, lost on the map, ignoring the voice that insisted, *Turn back, turn back. Go back inside the house. Don't go that way, don't go there.*

I squeezed my eyes shut. The edges of the town disintegrated and I sank. My focus became closer, shorter, then back to real life. I opened my eyes to the present. The garage. My bike.

My father thought I had a natural talent, a "gift" he called it, which embarrassed me, like I was in one of those movies where kids see dead people or predict the future or whatever. It was part knack for gauging distances, part photographic memory of geospatial imagery.

Sometimes it felt like a curse. Sometimes I got lost in it. Sometimes I could see less clearly what was right in front of me than I could see a landscape, miles away. It would start with one fixed point, like the garage—then, as if I were floating straight up, the surrounding area would grow and grow. The grid of roads, the borders of the towns. The colors of states, the dark blue oceans, the countries, the continents. I could measure the distances between that first point and everything surrounding it, no matter how high I climbed or how far the borders spread.

Sometimes I felt like I couldn't land. And sometimes I didn't want to.

• • •

I'd first discovered how good I was at mapping distances when my cat went missing. I was ten. I'd had Bootsy since she was a kitten, and she slept on my pillow at night, and sometimes (well, a lot of the time) I gave her canned tuna fish as a special treat. She had a good life, so I couldn't understand why she would leave me, leave *us*.

In truth, she was probably run over by a car or eaten by a coyote. Or worse, caught in a rabbit trap. But at the time Dad didn't have the heart to tell me the likely possibilities, so he accompanied me as I went around the town, taping up LOST CAT posters wherever I could. I cried a lot. When I closed my eyes, I would see Bootsy in the woods, scared and cold and alone.

"She'll find her way home one day," Dad would say, trying to soothe me at night.

He would stroke my hair back from my forehead as I lay in bed, crying into the pillow. He told me that cats had an inner compass. When lost, cats would lie down and feel a tug inside them, like a fish on a line, toward home.

While I was still looking for Bootsy, MapOut was starting up. My dad had decided to document all the footpaths in the Amherst woods—long abandoned—to demonstrate the company's capabilities to potential clients. He brought me along when he could. I spent my time calling for Bootsy while he marked the trees with red or blue or yellow paint. Sometimes I would hold his compass in my hand, close my eyes, and spin myself around until I got so dizzy that I had to collapse on the damp forest floor. Then, like a cat, I would try to feel the pull of each direction.

I assigned them colors in my head. South was orange, north

was green, west was pale blue, and east was purple. With my eyes closed, I laid the compass beside me and saw everything. The colors became indistinguishable from the different pulls I felt. When I opened my eyes and checked the compass, everything matched up. I never missed.

I told my dad. He kind of smiled and said, "You're lucky, sweetheart."

But I knew it was more than that. When I began to tell him that he'd gotten the distances wrong between the paint markings—it wasn't thirty yards; it was actually thirty yards and eight inches—he sat me down and looked at me. "Tanya," he whispered. "I'm telling you this for your own good. I am so sorry, but I really think that Bootsy is dead."

I burst into tears and ran straight home.

After that, I never told anyone else about my ability, not even Beth. I guess it did seem kind of strange. The feeling and certainty I had about direction and distances couldn't be summed up with words, anyway. It was all a map in my head, an invisible feline tug. And Dad knew that. He knew I shared with Piri Reis whatever trait had allowed him to map the earth as if staring down from thousands of miles up in space.

But only later did I realize that Dad had told me the awful truth about Bootsy for a simple reason: to protect me.

I gripped my bike's handlebars, ignoring the pain in my hand as I sped down the road into town. I drew a series of deep, shaky breaths. "Pull yourself together, Tanya," I said to myself. But I couldn't. I slammed on the brakes, jolting forward.

A bicyclist behind swerved around me. "Watch what

you're doing!" she screamed over her shoulder. Her voice reminded me of Rebs. I knew it wasn't her, though. If it had been Rebs, she would have leapt off the bike and swept me into a hug. Or slapped me. Or pleaded with me to crawl out of my shell. Anyway, Rebs was off at Camp Norwich. "Sorry," I stammered. I unfastened my helmet. Once I'd stopped trembling, I threw it down on the concrete, reveling in the crack of the plastic against the road. *I should have stayed with Beth. I should have never taken this internship in the first place.*

After my mother died, after the funeral—after the mourners had left their bright bouquets and the well-wishers had dropped off their baked goods and casseroles—I was filled with a sadness so heavy I could barely stand the weight of it. I knew she was dead. But I was young, and I still believed in heaven. The funeral had sent her on her way. I would lie on my bed sending kisses up to the sky.

For my father there was no funeral, no ashes, or burial. Only a stiff memorial. Wilted flowers at an empty gravesite.

He was killed on a mapping expedition in Cambodia. I remember very clearly how Harrison had tried to stop him from going, warning that the trip was too dangerous; besides, MapOut didn't have the money to cover his insurance. The countryside was still pocked with land mines. The area was impossibly remote. The argument marked the first real rift between them, and their last: the natural culmination of long-brewing tension.

When it came down to it, Dad had partnered with Harrison because he loved the art and adventure of cartography. But Harrison was a businessman. There was no commerce in rural Cambodia, no lucrative "demographic" MapOut could target with advertisers. Advertising ruled at MapOut. It paid the bills. Exploring the unknown for exploration's sake did not.

Dad went anyway, of course. He even used one of Harrison's business strategies against him: Harrison's portrayal of Dad as the "brand" of the company. The rugged genius. The lone pioneer. The old-fashioned cartographer, documenting the uncharted until every inch of Earth could be known and seen. Wasn't that MapOut's promise? Harrison himself had turned Michael Barrett into its poster child, and this trip proved he was living up to the image . . . which by definition meant it was good for business, regardless of risk or cost.

Cambodia. I could picture what had happened. Dad had strayed from the team with his compass and measuring stick. Because in the end, Harrison was right about Michael Barrett: that was what he did; that was what made him who he was. He'd wandered out of cell range—if there had even been any at all—off the GPS and satellite locators. And then he was caught in a flash flood, gone in an instant.

There was nothing left of him. His team eventually found a waterlogged notebook, the ink so smeared across the page that it looked like a watercolor painting. A few days later, the baseball hat from his college days turned up several miles downstream: his good-luck charm.

The only other remnant of the tragedy is satellite footage of the water cresting over the riverbanks. I watched it with Harrison and Beth after Harrison broke the news, all of us in tears. Everything just goes blue, though. You don't hear my dad's cries for help; you don't even see him—the resolution isn't sharp enough. In stillness and silence, death seems painless. The water rises and recedes, taking my father with it.

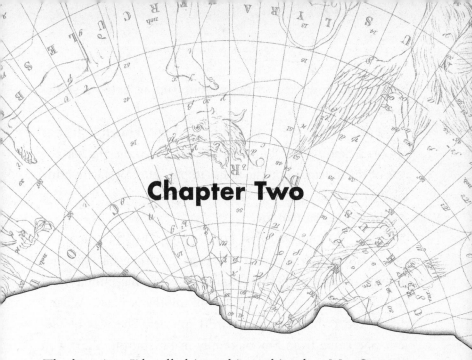

Chapter Two

The last time I'd pulled into this parking lot, MapOut was still small-time, occupying only the third floor. In the past six months it had taken over the entire building. Much of it was under new construction. I could hardly recognize it as the old paper-manufacturing plant, built of stately red brick, perched on the banks of the Mill River and renovated a decade earlier for an impending boom.

That boom seemed to have arrived.

I *knew* that things were going well. There had been some big acquisition by a major tech company, Rytech International. Harrison had explained it all to me even though I didn't care. All I remembered from that conversation was that Harrison felt guilty. Right after Dad died, he'd offered Beth a deal: she could sell my dad's shares in MapOut or keep them. Harrison told her there was a good chance that the company might sink, and I knew he believed it. If MapOut failed, we would be left with nothing except bankruptcy lawyers. Beth agreed to the payout and accepted a settlement for $350,000.

At the time, she was head-over-heels grateful. It was almost sickening. But I understood her gratitude. She had the rest of the mortgage on the house to pay, plus all the monthly bills on a kindergarten teacher's salary.

Plus taking care of me.

When she and Dad first hooked up, I was just Internet-savvy enough to research every part of her background, hoping to find something scandalous or incriminating. I still didn't want anyone taking my mother's place. What I discovered only made me weirdly angrier. She was blameless. She came from a poor family in Pittsburgh. She'd won a scholarship and put herself through UMass, where she got an advanced degree in Early Childhood Education. And then she'd come to Amherst to teach kindergarten.

Needless to say, she used the settlement money to pay off the mortgage; she paid off her car loan; she put a chunk into a seven-year CD that would be mine after college. But she could have had so much more, and Harrison knew it now—but only after the fact, after this big company had swooped in after his partner's death and saved his struggling start-up. Maybe that was why he was so insistent that I take this internship.

Staring up at the scaffold, I felt a flash of anger at Dad. He should have listened to Harrison. He should have lived long enough to see the company's sudden success. I still remembered how he and Harrison would work from the office in our house with only one intern—an Amherst junior named Fred, glued to the screen, hunchbacked, with thick glasses, always guzzling Coca-Cola.

As I made my way to the parking lot, I spotted Harrison's black Audi station wagon sparkling under the sunlight. I wondered if I could put my bike on the roof. There was no room on the general rack, already crowded with the bikes of the other paid interns from Amherst, UMass, Hampshire, and Smith.

One of the reasons MapOut stayed in this area was because of the inexpensive intelligence. "Ivy League brains at sweatshop prices," Harrison liked to say, thinking he was being funny. He was always oblivious to how offensive he sounded. That was another difference between him and Dad, and one that I wish Dad would have called him on more.

As I hesitated, a car pulled into the lot, a navy-blue Jetta. The windows were rolled down, and music spilled out into the sun.

I spotted a Stanford University sticker on the rear windshield.

Connor. My stomach squeezed. I was half tempted to turn around and pedal away. How had I forgotten that Harrison's son would be a part of the MapOut operation this summer? He and I had been friends when we were young—playmates, really, thrown together while our fathers worked or hung out—until he left for boarding school. Then we lost touch. Or more like he lost touch with me. Screw it; if I was completely honest with myself (and there was no reason not to be), I could admit the truth: he'd hurt me. Even before boarding school, he'd put distance between us. I hadn't seen him in three years, not since that summer before ninth grade.

Pretending not to notice him, I walked my bike into a shady spot beneath the trees. The engine died. The music stopped. A car door opened and closed. I stood still, gripping the handlebars of my bike, hoping I was camouflaged.

"Tanya!"

I still recognized his voice, but it was deeper now. I gripped the handles of my bike tighter. There was no use ignoring him.

"Hey, Tanya!" he shouted again, louder.

I wanted to act surprised but casual, but my eyes widened when I looked up. He was nearly a spitting image of his father. His face was narrower, and somehow softer, too, punctuated by bright green eyes. He'd grown a little under five inches since I'd last seen him; he was six-one now. His shoulders were broader, so the messy brown "I'm-in-college" mop hair finally made sense. His jaw had lost its baby fat. He wore jeans, grey sneakers, and a navy T-shirt with STANFORD UNIVERSITY printed across the front.

"Hey!" he yelled with a smile, running to catch up to me.

"Hey," I said.

"How are you?" He met my gaze, then avoided it, then met it again. His smile faltered. "My dad told me you'd be working here. I'm just . . . I want to say I'm sorry about your dad. I wish I could have been at the service."

"Thanks." I nodded, then stopped myself, wondering why I was nodding. I suddenly felt overwhelmed with self-consciousness, imagining how I looked to him. The pathetically sad figure, the orphaned daughter of his dad's dead best friend. My bike helmet was fastened tightly beneath my chin, my school backpack on, my pants tucked into my socks so they didn't get caught in the bike's gears. Were my armpits sweaty?

"Anyway, it's nice to see you," he said. "It's been a while."

"Three years." I wasn't sure why I needed to clarify. Then

things got worse. The Velcro on my helmet stuck to my hair as I tried to pull it from my head.

"Hey, let me help you," he offered.

"It's okay. I'm used to it. This happens all the time. Sometimes I just leave my helmet hanging from my hair all day so I won't lose it."

He laughed and walked up beside me, gently tugging my hair loose from the knotted strap, then handed me the helmet. "There."

"Thanks." I'd managed to get one pant leg free from my sock. I was working on the other when my backpack fell off my shoulder. I imagined myself back at home with Beth, sobbing into her pillow as the birds chirped. It didn't seem so bad.

"So my dad really convinced you to take the internship," he said. He sounded as if he were talking to himself.

"It's good for college," I said, sounding like a robot.

"I guess it is. That's why I took it. Résumé-building. I . . ." He drew in a breath.

"What?" I asked, feeling even more self-conscious.

He smiled slightly. "I'm just glad you said that, too. Honestly I wanted to intern for Habitat for Humanity. I was all set to go to Tanzania and help on this well-building project, but Dad seems to think this internship will be better for 'my future' . . ." He broke off again, maybe embarrassed at how he'd managed both to put down his dad and extol his own virtues. "Never mind."

"So, where *do* you go to college, anyway?" I said. I gestured to his T-shirt. I don't know why I felt the need to make fun of him. On the other hand, his perfection practically begged for it.

His cheeks turned pink. "It was the only clean shirt I had."

"I was just kidding." My voice was weak. I felt a pinch in my ribs—why did I say that just to be mean? Now I was the bitter, mean orphan. Wonderful.

At least he gave up any pretenses of being chipper. "Have you been inside yet? They're completely remodeling."

I shook my head.

"Come on. I'll show you around."

The air inside was dusty, barely breathable. Connor led me up cement stairs past the first two floors, cordoned off under heavy plastic construction drapes, to where the original office had been. A young woman with very pale white skin and a dyed-black bob sat on the phone at a long white desk. Above her hung a banner of glowing lights spelling MapOut. Her red sandals tapped the floor as she typed the caller's information into the computer. "Harrison is in a meeting at the moment . . ."

On the other side of the large room were office cubicles. I saw a bunch of kids barely older than me, typing away: Harrison's collegiate sweatshop brain trust. Brand-new boxes of unopened Macs stood against the wall. A team of deliverymen were assembling Knoll furniture—red and orange chairs, white round tables. For a second I was dizzy. Rytech International must have given MapOut more money than I'd even imagined. No wonder Harrison felt guilty. This *was* the same floor the old office had occupied, but it had been completely redone. It was unrecognizable.

Connor ushered me past the receptionist to a pair of double glass doors and knocked lightly. Harrison had a private suite now. I wondered what had happened to my father's old office, what had happened to his equipment.

"Come in," Harrison called.

I'm not sure why, but my eyes began to sting. That gravelly tone, that slight Boston accent; I had grown up with this voice. Connor nudged me inside.

Harrison was already hurrying around a vast mahogany desk. He wore a grey linen suit with a white T-shirt beneath. He opened his arms wide to sweep me into the warm, familial hug he always did.

"Tanya, hello. I've got that college trust set up for you. I'll take you out to lunch one day this week and we can talk about it," he murmured. Then he stepped back and gave my shoulder a gentle squeeze. I could smell the watery spice scent of his aftershave. "All you have to do is get grades again like you used to."

I nodded with a half smile. *Business first.* That was his way. "Connor, I want you to show Tanya the data input she'll be doing. I have a lunch meeting in Boston." He glanced quickly at the stainless-steel chain-link watch hanging from his wrist.

"Sure, Dad," Connor said, his voice equally abrupt.

"How's Beth doing?" he asked.

At first I wasn't sure if Harrison was talking to me. He texted a message on his phone, then slipped it into his suit pocket.

"She's okay," I said. "She got the roof fixed finally so it's not leaking. She's thinking about going back to work . . ." What I really wanted to ask was, How could MapOut afford this huge renovation? How much was the Rytech acquisition worth?

Harrison's eyes locked with mine. I could tell right away that the settlement was a subject he wanted to avoid. I flashed again to last winter and Beth's eager acceptance. I knew Harrison was only trying to protect us, but I was sure that giving up wasn't what Dad would have wanted. He never had intentions of cashing out his stock. But I had no legal rights and could not convince Beth, who was now my sole guardian.

"So, Connor, you're Tanya's boss today," Harrison finished with a paternal wink. He buttoned his suit coat and grabbed his briefcase.

The pale receptionist appeared, handing him a note on MapOut letterhead: a name and phone number. A smile crept across my lips. They'd changed the font but kept the slogan my dad and I had come up with one night hanging out in the shed. *MapOut: Put Yourself on the Map.*

Connor walked me to the last empty cubicle. "You're going to need coffee," he said impishly.

"I will?" I asked, surveying the empty desk and blank screen.

"Trust me. People like you and me get stuck with data entry." He was already walking away, waving me down a narrow corridor. I sighed and followed. "Do you know about FYF? The new app they're working on here?"

"Find Your Friends, right? My dad mentioned something about it." I closed my mouth before I could add: *before he died.* I really needed to shut off that part of my brain, the part that triggered a painful memory every single time his name came up. But I could picture the excited smile on his face as he told me about its implications—about how it would take location-based technology to a whole new level. *"Nobody*

*will ever have to be afraid of getting lost in a strange crowd
or a new city,"* he'd said more than once. *"We're so close to
being safe no matter where we are. Isn't that something?"*

"Yeah, my dad is riding everyone extra hard so he can roll
it out by Christmas," Connor said in the silence.

"Is that what I'm going to be working on?" I asked.

He sighed. "I wish. Like I said, right now we're only
assigned to data entry. But you never know, maybe someday."

Unlike my cubicle, the kitchen was bright and airy. A
cappuccino maker and French press filled with newly made
coffee sat on the counter. Fair trade, Organic Dark Roast
Sumatra Rao's Coffee beans stored in airtight jars.

"Caffeine is sacred here, huh?" I asked.

"You'll understand why soon enough." Connor poured
me a cup.

I added half-and-half and stirred until it was a rich caramel
color. A few scruffy programmer types shuffled in and out.
He made a point to introduce me: "This is Tanya, Michael's
daughter." Everyone was friendly—preoccupied, but friendly.
I didn't remember a single name. Still, for the first time since
I'd agreed to work here, I thought my summer might turn out
okay. At least I'd forgotten being hurt by my former childhood friend.

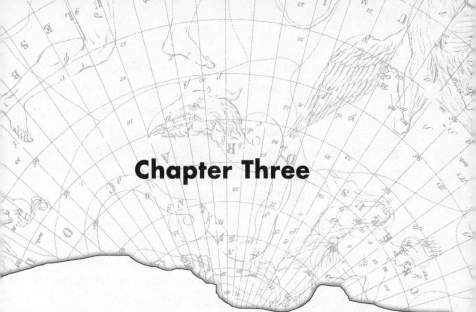

Chapter Three

Connor wasn't kidding. My job was to type very boring information into a database. But then, I already knew that MapOut's primary mission was boring: to create an application that was both a shoppers' map and a business owners' tool.

The first folder I picked up was for a neighborhood in South Carolina called District 8. I was meant to input a breakdown of flower shop data. For instance: Florence's Flowers on Chestnut Drive charged $22.00 for a dozen roses. If you drove five miles south out of town, The Yellow Daffodil charged only $21.50.

The data MapOut gathered was constantly changing, with new information being updated. So if you, the customer, went to Florence's Flowers and you were dissatisfied, you could search the MapOut app with a command like: "Locate flower shop within five miles that sells a dozen roses for under $22." Of course, the ultimate goal, the one that consumed all the young programmers, was to cut out typing altogether. At the end of the summer the new-and-improved version was due to be released: you would just hit the MapOut button, hovering somewhere on your screen over the Florence's Flowers page, and all the information you'd need about a better place to buy flowers would appear.

After ten minutes, I could no longer concentrate.

I kept trying to figure out exactly where I was in the building—the way I remembered it—but everything was blocked off. Makeshift drywalls blocked hallways; heavy sheets of dark plastic covered exits and entrances; doors were sealed shut.

Connor must have been spying on me, because he pulled up a chair. He began pestering me about how the work was going, if I was finding the system difficult to navigate. I shooed him away, not even realizing how rude I was being. I felt bad, but I couldn't explain to him how I was feeling, the overwhelming necessity to locate myself in a place that had once been so familiar. I needed to figure out where I was. Like the arrow on a map that says, YOU ARE HERE. *Here* is something I always have to know.

And there was something else that had been needling at me since I'd arrived: my dad's office. There was a chance it might have already been gutted in the renovation. If it hadn't, though, his desktop computer might still be inside.

For some reason, Harrison couldn't give us Dad's computer. Beth had asked for it, mostly because it was handy to have another computer in the house. But apparently Harrison's hands were tied. His lawyers couldn't allow it. Dad's computer was officially company property and contained company information and data. If we took possession of it, we'd set a "dangerous precedent."

Beth had agreed, of course. And Harrison was probably right about corporate data. Once, he'd even been forced to come to the house—I'd never seen him look less suave and confident—apologizing over and over and asking if either Beth or I knew a password Dad might have used for business emails. Beth, always eager to please, took a small brown notebook from Dad's desk drawer and handed it over to Harrison. I don't think Dad would have minded, but still, it felt like a violation. Dad was a cofounder of the company; didn't that mean we could inherit the computer? Besides, his notebook certainly didn't qualify as MapOut property.

I sat in the cubicle for a few more minutes, sipping my coffee, staring blankly at the monitor: a pale grey blur of symbols and codes. The college student at the cubicle beside me was singing along softly to the music playing in his headphones. Steeling my nerves, I pushed my chair out behind me, quietly. I would use my usual excuse: *Oh, I was just looking for the bathroom.* Or if that was too obvious I would just pretend I was on my way back to the kitchen to refill my coffee.

I picked up the nearly empty coffee cup. I put my earphones in to discourage people from talking to me. From where I stood, I could see north down the hall to what I knew was once the stairwell. The banister and doorway were smothered in heavy plastic and blocked with piles of construction sheetrock, making access beyond that point impossible. So: another route. Heading to the back of the building, I lingered by the side of the freight elevator and stared down at my phone, pretending to be distracted just in case one of workmen asked me what I was doing. I acted as if I belonged here, as if I were caught up in important texts—oblivious to where I was and who was around me.

"It's so easy to play stupid and snoop nowadays. People have lost that instinct for exploration. The only thing they seem to be interested in exploring are their smartphones. That's something we mapmakers can use to our advantage."

Dad's words rang as clearly as if he'd spoken out loud.

When I was a kid, out exploring with him—mapping the trails Native Americans used centuries ago—he'd encourage me to snoop. Originally the land was everyone's to travel and explore; now the trees were posted with PRIVATE PROPERTY and NO TRESPASSING signs. Needless to say, Dad didn't respect those boundaries, especially if it interfered with cartography. The trails were mostly overgrown, blending into the woods as though they had never been there. When we came across a grumpy landowner (sometimes with a deer-hunting rifle), we'd just pretended to be lost. Bird-watching, blueberry-picking, following a fox trail: these were all excuses I learned to use.

The elevator opened and I stepped inside, pulling the heavy doors closed. There were no buttons to press, only a lever. I turned it the only possible way—to the left—and felt the slow rise of the cables pulling upward. It was dark; only single strand of light shone through the seam.

The elevator slammed into the ceiling. The back of my head hit the wall. *Shit.*

Slowly, steadily, I lowered the lever an inch at a time, gauging from the seam of light when I'd linked to the fourth floor. Then I pulled open the doors and stepped into a broad, empty space. My eyes zeroed in on the emergency staircase:

access to the blocked-off area of the third floor. The next thing I knew, I was jogging down the steps.

This was the old MapOut.

The original sign still hung over the entrance to the shabby suite of rooms. The first thing I recognized was the smell of old wood and clay from the pottery studio that used to be next door. But that studio had long been dismantled to make more room for MapOut. An unpleasant thought flitted through my mind: Had Harrison been lying when he'd told Beth and me the company was in jeopardy? Had he already known about Rytech and the obvious millions they were willing to supply?

It was best not to go there. He'd always looked out for me, and he still did. I pulled my earphones out. I hurried toward my father's office.

The floors in the old section were worn and uneven in places. The cubicles were silent, relics from another era compared to the new, glossy white ones downstairs. The printer was covered with dust. There was a pile of printing paper on the desk; pens; paper clips. My throat tightened. The last time I had been here, Dad was alive. I would walk here after school and do my homework while he finished work.

The poster of the Piri Reis map was still tacked into the door.

I reached for the handle and tried to turn it, but it was locked. The map blurred in front of me. I had sworn to myself I wouldn't cry about this anymore. I didn't hear the approaching footsteps. I didn't hear anything at all. I was just trying to stop the tears. I squeezed my eyes shut so tightly that I saw red—until a voice cut through.

"Tanya?" Connor was jogging down the dusty hallway.

"What are you doing here? No one's supposed to be in this area. It's not safe."

My face flushed. I turned my back to him, trying to wipe my cheeks as quickly as possible. My mind was racing, but I knew no excuse would work.

"I just wanted to see my dad's office," I confessed.

Maybe he didn't hear. I barely heard my own voice. I shut my eyes again and leaned against the wall feeling weak, and hating myself for that weakness. I slid down to the floor. Everything was quiet for a moment. Maybe he had taken the hint and gone. Then I heard his voice again, closer this time. I opened my eyes. He was staring at the Piri Reis map with a faraway look.

"I should have figured you'd come up here. I . . . I'm sorry," he said. "I know you've been through a lot."

Thanks. You can leave now.

But he didn't. He sat down beside me on the floor. Neither of us spoke. I could hear him breathing. And I knew he could hear me crying, even as I tried to hold back.

"You know, there was something I wanted to tell you, something I actually thought about writing to you before this summer," he said. "But then, I don't know. It didn't seem like the right time. There *is* no right time. It's just . . . your dad was a big inspiration for me. He said something to me that always stuck. 'No matter where I end up, I'm always right where I want to be, because it's new.'"

I kept silent. If Connor had intended to torture me, he was doing an excellent job. This was my punishment for wandering away from my cubicle. A tear splattered on the dusty floor between us. He pretended not to notice.

"Anyway, that was the reason I got involved in Habitat

for Humanity," Connor added. "It was right after he died.
Maybe it was even . . . I don't know. But when I signed up,
I pictured him with his backpack. I loved how he would
just trek off and do his own thing. I loved how you could
tell that he hated everything my dad loves, all the apps and
technology and bullshit schmoozing. All he cared about was
experience."

I sniffed and shook my head. "I know, Connor," I whispered, my voice hoarse. "In the end that's what killed him.
He should have been more like your dad, sitting behind a
desk."

He let out a grim laugh. "Who wants to do that?"

For a while we were silent again.

"Hey, you know what?" he said. "I'm serious. It's summer
break. I don't want to spend it typing in the price of Nike
Airs in Westville, Ohio, do you?"

I frowned at him. The silly smile on his face made me
laugh and cry again at the same time.

"My dad's heading to Boston. He might have already split.
I really doubt anyone's going to notice if we take a lunch
break now. Come on." He stood and nudged me lightly with
his foot. "I'm sure if you eat something and get an iced tea—
my treat. I mean . . . look. I know nothing I do or say will
make you actually feel better about your dad. It is what it is.
It sucks. But distractions can help."

I blinked up at him. He had said something so true.
He probably didn't realize it, but he was the first person
in my life to actually say it out loud: *Nothing would
make me better.* And the relief of someone giving me
the hard truth, as painful as it might be, was so much

more refreshing than hearing the same old time-heals-all-wounds bullshit.

"You know, you're the first person who has said something real about what happened to my dad," I said.

Our eyes met before he looked away, as though he were embarrassed about what he might add.

"I . . . Sorry about that," he stuttered. I could tell he was straining for the right words. "Sometimes stuff pops out of my mouth. When my parents split, Mom pretty much left me, too. Did you know that? She only visited me four times at Exeter, same time every year: Parent Weekend. I kept trying to do things to get her attention like get good grades or play on varsity, even in ninth grade." His voice caught in his throat.

Of course I had known about the divorce, that his mother had moved to New York City with her boyfriend and his daughters. But I had no idea she'd abandoned him.

After he left for Exeter (*of course, only the best for Connor*), I'd assumed he thought he was better than everyone. Every report that came back was confirmation: straight A's, amazing athlete, handsome. There was even a rumor going around that he was dating some heiress. He seemed non-human, a machine. And in a way he was: a machine devoted to getting his own mother to notice him.

I hesitated, but I couldn't help ask, "Did she even come to your graduation?"

"Yeah. So, five times, I guess. But that was awkward because Dad was there, too. I haven't seen her since, and she's never visited me at college. She was supposed to visit but something came up, something about her new boyfriend . . . whatever. I'm

used to her excuses now. I never expect anything anymore."
He turned abruptly. "Come on. Look how sunny and bright it
is outside. Let's go. I'm taking you out to lunch."

I looked up at him wearily. "Easy for you to say, you're the
boss's son."

"Exactly," he said with a smirk. "I can do whatever I
want."

"Connor . . ." I had to laugh. "Listen, this is a shit situation for me, but I do need this job right now. We have to walk
right past the receptionist to get out."

He smiled. "Yeah, but we're not going out the front door."

Chapter Four

The back fire escape shook as I stepped out onto the window ledge.

I looked down four flights of rusted iron ladders and grates to the ground below, imagining my body tumbling through the air.

"It's fine," Connor said. He held out his hand. "I'll go first to prove it."

I gripped the railing with both hands. Maybe all fire escapes wobbled? Holding my breath, I took his hand in mine. A vivid memory overcame me: doing the exact same thing when we were seven years old, behind my house. My mom had still been alive. He'd stepped onto a log in the river and reached out for me to join him . . .

It must have only been three or four seconds, but when he let go and turned back to the railing, it was as though I had lost something—I'd been shown a keepsake only to have it snatched away. But that wasn't *his* fault. I made my way down the steep and narrow steps, following his lead. At the bottom landing, he jumped on the ladder, which slid to the ground with a thud. I climbed down after him, stepping onto the gravel. After that he grabbed the bottom rung and shoved hard—and the ladder slid back into place, suspended over our heads.

"Little trick I learned a couple of days ago," he said slyly.

Now we were at the back of the building, hidden by the scaffold, away from the parking lot. I peered around to see if Harrison's car was still there. Across from us was a one-way road, beyond that, the bike path through the woods.

Connor signaled. We both broke into a sprint—not stopping after we'd crossed the road; all the windows of the MapOut building faced the bike path. We ducked into the woods and kept going. After a hundred yards, after the brush had gotten too thick to run, I stopped to catch my breath.

I gazed up through the branches and treetops at the clear blue sky. The air felt cooler and damp; it smelled of pine and the particular whiff of sun on wood. How many times had I looked up like this? Hundreds, thousands, but every time the sky managed to appear beautiful and new. Maybe only because I was most comfortable picturing myself up there in the clouds, staring down.

I turned to Connor. Both of us were still panting from the run. Our eyes caught and he turned away, quickly glancing down at the ground. We stood for a moment in what felt like an awkward silence.

"Tanya?" he gasped.

"Yeah."

"Remember how we used to play together out by that river behind your house, when we were kids?"

I nodded. So he'd remembered, as well. My face flushed a little. "It feels a little like that," I managed.

We also spent time indoors. We spied on our parents. We could be alone and together at the same time . . . There was so much more I could add. Up in the attic, I'd studied atlases and globes and computer screens. He'd stayed with the toys, building robots and strange rockets with tentacles and wheels that could land on faraway planets. Whatever we'd done, we'd felt comfortable enough to spend time together without having to talk. That was what made his disappearance all the more hurtful. The silence had become permanent.

"You moved," I said. "I wrote you a letter once . . . I think?" I tried to sound vague but I remembered it all so clearly: writing the address in New York City, inscribing each number of the zip code so the mailman would be able to read it. And how I sealed the envelope with my tongue and a glow-in-the-dark sticker of a star. "Did you ever get it?" My voice sounded strange even to me. High-pitched and unsure.

I waited for him to answer. I heard my heart thumping. I felt it in my throat. *So did you? Did you get the letter I spent days composing? Wasted my entire set of Crane stationery on rewrites? Did you?*

Connor finally shrugged and flashed a smile like his dad's. "Yeah. I'm pretty sure I did. I was just going through a lot with the divorce and everything."

I kept my face perfectly still. *Then why didn't you write back? I could have been there for you. Why didn't you ever keep in touch? Because telling me you wanted to write me about Dad but never did feels like a cop-out.*

"No big deal," I said, using my not-caring-or-paying-attention voice.

"Cool," he said.

I almost felt like applauding myself. I was wasting my time with this MapOut internship. I should have been an actress.

After we'd put enough distance between ourselves and MapOut, we found our way back to the bike path and headed toward Amherst College. It was noon and only a few cyclists were out. It felt as though we had this gorgeous day all to ourselves, that it belonged only to us.

"I saw Beth the other day," Connor said.

"My stepmother, Beth?"

He nodded thoughtfully, his eyes on the packed dirt. "She was in the office having lunch with my dad. She's the one who told me you'd be working here this summer."

I stopped short. "She was at the office? Why?"

Connor turned to me. "Um, probably because she was married to your dad?" He was smiling, but his forehead was creased.

"Right." I kept walking, not liking the way my voice had sounded. Still, I was annoyed that Beth had been hanging around the MapOut offices. Would she be there this summer? Checking up on me, like she always did? I couldn't stop myself from asking in the exact same voice: "I guess Beth likes to trek off on her own, too, huh?"

He sighed. "I knew I shouldn't have said anything . . ."

"No, I'm sorry." I almost reached out to touch his arm, but stopped.

"You know, what I really meant to say just now is that I'm sorry I didn't answer your letter." He glanced at me out of the corner of his eye. "I miss those times when we were kids. I miss when your dad and my dad would argue."

I frowned. "You do?"

Connor cracked a smile and tried to hide it. "Yeah. Your dad would put my dad in his place. Nobody really does that anymore."

"How do you mean?"

"You know . . . the way your dad would try to make a case that maps should be free to whoever wanted them. 'People can't *own* maps any more than they can own truth!'" Connor quoted in an eerily dead-on imitation of my father. "He actually said that. Maps were just a form of truth. My dad would be like, 'Are you crazy? Why would we share our data for free when we could sell it?'" Connor's eyes darkened. He shook his head and shoved his hands in his pockets.

"What?" I pressed, suddenly caught up in Connor's memory.

"Nothing," he mumbled. "You know what I liked most about your dad? He hated texting. He was always ranting to my dad about having real conversations or just not using the phone at all. I'm the same way. I hate the phone. I hate texting."

I processed the words. There were so many ways I could have answered, so many directions I could take *this* conversation. Was Connor trying to comfort me in some way because he still felt guilty that he hadn't reached out to me when my dad had died? Did he hate the phone because of *his* dad? Harrison's fortune was built on phone technology. Did Connor really want to help build wells in Tanzania? Was that why he was always so weirdly coiled and distant and attentive at the same time, as if one step away from pouncing on something? Because he truly wanted a "real" experience, like my dad? Because he knew he had to pounce on something if he got the chance?

But what popped out of my mouth was: "So where are we going, anyway?"

As we walked past the tennis courts of Amherst College and along Main Street I felt happy, lit up inside in a way I hadn't since Dad was alive. I knew part of it was because of Connor, but I would never admit that fully, not even to myself. I hadn't realized how much I'd missed him until today; I hadn't even allowed myself to think about him. But he'd shared a part of my life no one ever would or could, the part where I'd been the third member of a family—the best part, those years before Mom died.

"*Three is a magic number,*" she used to sing to me, even in the hospital when she was sick: an old kids' song from her youth, about two parents with an only child.

Connor reminded me of being that number three; he brought that feeling back. Just being around him anchored me to my past. I don't think he had any idea that I missed him when he moved away or how much I cared about him. I also guessed he really didn't need to know. Besides, he probably wouldn't understand even if I ever tried to tell him.

I wasn't surprised that he chose The Black Sheep Café, on Main Street, across from the common. It was an Amherst institution, crowded with students: pita-bread hippie-veggie sandwiches with crazy names, bottomless coffee, oversized double chocolate cupcakes. We stood in line, reading aloud the names of sandwiches from the blackboard, debating. In the end we ordered two Herbivores and two iced coffees with milk—and a black-and-white cookie to share.

Connor insisted on paying, so I let him. Usually I would have argued and insisted on splitting the bill, thinking that's what being an independent/modern/feminist type of girl was about. This time I didn't argue too much. Besides, what did I have to prove? He was the richer of us. No doubt his dad handed him a hefty allowance. Not to mention that Harrison was now sole owner of the company—a company that had skyrocketed in value since my dad's death and days as a partner there . . .

Obviously I wasn't bitter.

We found a table for two in the back of the café. A middle-aged man with a long, brown beard, receding hair—in too-short cutoffs and tie-dyed T-shirt—played acoustic Grateful Dead covers on his guitar. All I noticed were his uncut toenails poking out of his Birkenstocks. Sometimes this town felt like a caricature of itself: a mixture of '60s-era hippies and preppy college students wanting to be associated with . . . this guy.

Connor's phone buzzed on the table. Before he could grab it, the image of a girl appeared on the screen. FaceTime. The girl had long, straight, bright blonde hair (too bright in my opinion), a perfect smile. I only glanced for a second but I saw her name, ISABEL CHASE, light up across the screen.

"Thinking of you ;)"

I called FaceTime "UglyTime." That's what it felt like whenever I used it but Isabel actually looked pretty on the screen.

He grabbed the phone, pressed IGNORE, and put it facedown on the table. A few seconds later, the phone buzzed again.

"Who's Isabel?"

"How's your sandwich?" he replied.

"Is she your girlfriend?"

Connor looked up with a flash of annoyance. "Another reason I hate the phone. Are you one of those people who'll ask about everyone who calls?"

"Why, is something wrong with that?"

"It's about privacy, that's all," he said.

I rolled my eyes. "Privacy? We work for a company whose business it is to map every millimeter of the Earth. Privacy goes out the window when it's impossible to get lost." I stared at him. "Isn't that part of why you wanted to go to Tanzania?"

He smirked. "Point made."

I couldn't resist persisting. "So, you didn't answer the question. Is she your girlfriend?"

Connor let out a sigh. "Isabel was in my freshman lit class. We sorta-kinda started seeing each other last semester."

"She's pretty," I said.

"Thanks."

An awkward few minutes ticked slowly by. Avoiding each other's eyes, we chewed our messy pitas and wiped our mouths with napkins. My stomach felt tight. I could barely taste the food. My phony confidence was fading into real embarrassment. Talking about his girlfriend was a no-no. But why? She was smart (she went to Stanford) and pretty (in the universal guy-taste way), and straight-white-teeth smiley (in a toothpaste-commercial way). If I were a guy I'd have been proud if she were my girlfriend. Why was he acting so cagey about the whole thing? Why would anybody try to hide something like that? Unless . . .

My mind jumped back to the conversation we'd had on the bike path.

"Wait," I said, thinking out loud. "Do you think Beth and Harrison are . . . ?" I wasn't sure how to phrase this, exactly. What would you use for middle-aged parents? Everything sounded seedy, gross. Hooking up? Dating? "Seeing each other?" I finished.

Connor sneered. "My dad and Beth? Are you kidding me? My dad only dates second-tier Victoria's Secret models."

"You mean he doesn't find the turtleneck/fleece/baggy jeans/clogs combo hot?" I was joking, but I felt a cold, sick feeling start in my stomach and spread into my throat. I'd never really trusted Beth. I'm not sure exactly why; she'd never been anything but good to me. Maybe it was because she was *too* good. Maybe it was the cloying way she showed up on our doorstep with lasagna and pies right after my mother died. Or the way she had sewn a lace collar on my favorite green sweatshirt, thinking I'd like it.

"Tanya—"

"Forget it," I interrupted. "I'm sure she had a good reason to be there."

Connor shifted in his chair uncomfortably. He reached for his coffee, taking a sip and glancing back at the hippie singer.

"What?" I asked.

"What do you mean, what?" he said.

"You're a crap liar. You always have been, even when we were kids. You're all fidgety now, which means you're hiding something."

He turned back to me and raised his eyebrows. "I didn't realize I was having lunch with an undercover FBI agent. Do you really want to know why Beth was at MapOut? She wanted access to your dad's private computer. She wanted to see the last emails he sent from work."

I blinked at him. "Did Harrison let her?"

"Yes. My dad wants access to his computer, too. I guess there's some company business he needs information about."

"So did Beth get in?"

Connor shook his head. "Nope. He triple-gated the encryption. Your dad was secretive—" He stopped himself. There was an edge in his voice.

I shoved my plate aside. "What are you saying?" I snapped. "He was trying to hide something from your dad?"

He swallowed. "Not from my dad," he muttered, avoiding my eyes. "I really didn't want to be the one to tell you this . . . Beth thinks he was having an affair."

"Oh, come on." I burst out laughing. "That's insane. Your dad's the affair type, not mine."

Connor leaned back. His lips pressed into a tight line.

What the hell was my problem? Not only had I said the wrong thing, I'd used a thoughtless insult as a weapon. I wished I could take it back. Harrison's affairs were what led to the divorce, which led to Connor moving away, which led to the ensuing custody battle where he was forced to take sides . . . and finally to the separation from his mother and his foray into being an über-achiever. All to win back the impossibly hard-to-get approval and attention he craved. In seconds, I'd turned his Achilles' heel into a glib joke.

"You need a filter," Connor said.

"I'm sorry."

He held my gaze under his bangs. "Anyway, I'm not the one who accused your dad of having an affair. It was Beth. That's why she wanted to see his emails."

I nodded. I had a sudden flashback to that wintry day when I saw the footsteps in the snow—so convinced my dad wasn't dead, so convinced that everything was normal. I could feel my flesh turning cold.

"Are you okay?" Connor asked, his voice softening.

"Yeah." I focused on him, shoving the pain from my mind. "It's just . . . someone came by our house last winter, someone who didn't want to be seen. I wonder if Beth asked your dad to snoop around on *my* dad."

Connor chewed his lip. "I don't know. I doubt it though."

I didn't think so, either, really. I couldn't imagine Harrison's doing anyone else's bidding but his own. But *someone* had wanted something from my dad. I leaned closer. "Listen. Can you get me into my dad's office? Then I can get into my dad's computer."

Connor flashed an amused smile. He mimicked me, leaning in, closing the distance between us, speaking in a hushed voice. "Just so you know, my dad had his three top computer guys try to hack in. Then he hired Blaze from MIT."

"Blaze?" I repeated. Clearly the name was supposed to mean something.

"A hacker. Never mind. He couldn't do it, either. Whoever your dad was emailing had serious security paranoia."

I nodded. "Got it, but I still want to try."

"Tanya—"

"Just let me try, okay? If my dad was having an affair, I want to know. You can understand that, can't you?"

His smile faded. Once again, he held my gaze. "I need you to promise me," he whispered in a low voice. "You can't tell anyone I did this."

I nodded, thrown by his intensity. "I won't. I swear." I held my hand out to shake on. He took my hand in his. He didn't shake it, but turned my palm upward. I felt his forefinger tracing letters in my palm: *P . . . R . . .*

It was something we used to do when we were kids, seated next to each other when we'd be trapped at dinner with our parents. I giggled as he continued. *O . . . M . . .* We'd finger-write messages to each other and stifle our laughter. *I . . . S . . .* Our hands were bigger now, of course, but the sensation brought back a flood of memories—swift and intense. I raised my eyes to meet his, feeling just a slight flush as I smiled.

"Promise," I whispered.

He traced the final *E* and held on for a moment, his finger lingering. Just like on the fire escape, I didn't want him to let go.

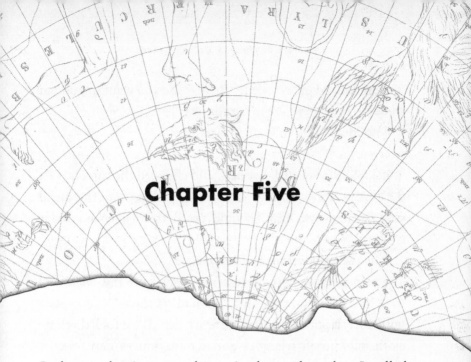

Chapter Five

Beth was planting green beans in the garden when I pulled my bike around the side of the house. She looked up at me, raising the brim on her straw sun hat.

"Hey there. How was your first day?"

I stood watching her, my backpack hanging from one shoulder. It was close to six. The early evening sun was still high above the western woods. "It was all right. I can't believe the renovation Harrison is doing. Have you seen it?"

Beth removed one of her gardening gloves and wiped her forehead with the back of her hand. "I've seen it. I . . . went there to talk to him."

So she passed the test; she'd admitted to being there, and more. Normally this would have been where I walked into the house, grabbed a snack from the kitchen, and locked my bedroom door behind me. Instead I asked, "Do you need any help?"

Beth looked up, startled. "Really? Do you want to pull out some carrots? If you're in for dinner?"

I nodded. "I'm in."

In the kitchen I peeled, washed, and chopped the carrots. I let the cool water wash over my hands, looking into the metal sink, strategizing how I would get Beth to open up about Connor's suspicions.

The oven timer rang, jolting me.

I turned to see Beth taking the quiche from the oven.

While I'd been at the sink, she had set the table, complete with a fresh pink peony from the garden. She'd folded yellow cloth napkins in triangles and set the knives and forks. I thought she did this type of thing only for my dad: the flower in the vase, the delicious-looking meal complete with decorative tomato and pinched pie crust. Maybe this was her way of showing me I was family, too. That we were all we had left.

"So I have a stack of summer reading I thought I could get away with sneaking at the internship . . . Did you ever read *The End of the Affair* by Graham Greene?"

I shoved a piece of lettuce into my mouth. Was I being too obvious? Dinner had been ten minutes of excruciating silence so far. Was there a way I could get her to tell me who she thought my dad was having an affair with? Or what I really wanted to know: if she'd recruited someone to snoop around his things after he'd passed away.

Beth put her fork down on her plate, making a clinking sound. She seemed to be staring at the wall. "*The End of the Affair*? Yes. It's one of my favorites."

I sipped some water. "I think Dad liked that book a lot. Well, I know he loved Graham Greene. You know what's weird that I've been thinking about?"

"What?" Beth smiled. Not a real smile, only a turn of her lips, weak and tired.

"Whenever Dad went away, he would send me an email. I mean even if it just said 'Hi, I'm in Cambodia' or whatever. Always an email, never a text . . . you know how he was. The other day I looked back at my emails from him and the last one he sent was five days before he died."

She touched the water glass, moving it an inch, then the silverware. This was a nervous habit of hers, rearranging things. I could tell there was something she was holding back. "He wasn't a fan of texting," she said in a tight voice.

I shrugged to ease the tension. "Maybe he just didn't have Internet access. He was in Cambodia. Did he send you any emails while he was there?"

Beth shook her head. "No, he didn't. To be honest, he'd been distant before he left." She looked as though she were about to say something else, then stopped herself. Her eyes met mine. "You were always the first person on his mind wherever he was."

I opened my mouth to protest. No words came. I hadn't been prepared for that. "Thanks," I whispered. "I'm sure you were, too."

"I wasn't." She squeezed her eyes shut, then stood, taking her plate and mine briskly to the sink. Her shoulders shook as she turned on the faucet.

"I'll clean up," I offered, not sure if she heard me over the water.

I knew she was crying. She must have known that I knew, because she hurried out of the room. There were footsteps on the stairs, followed by the sound of her bedroom door closing.

Night had already fallen when my phone dinged in my sweat-shirt pocket. My pulse beat a little quicker as I pulled it out.

Meet at Amherst Cinema 9 p.m.

A text from someone who hated texting. So it was impor-tant. I could guess what Connor was really telling me: he was going to get me into Dad's office. Tonight. It was already quarter past eight. I cleared the dishes from the table, rinsing and putting them in the dishwasher, and wiped the table clean. Then I hurried up the stairs to my bedroom, quickly changing out of the shorts I'd worn all day that were now dirty from the garden.

I rummaged through my drawers, all the while keeping an eye on the clock, before settling on a pair of jeans and my favorite navy-blue T-shirt. Once changed, I brushed my hair in the long mirror in the closet that, depending on how far the door was open, at times made you look tall and thin or short and squat. Tonight I opened it to the tall-and-thin angle to give myself the benefit of the doubt. Hair up? Hair down? This was the perpetual question. Down. Wait, no. Up. Up in a casual, high pony.

Then my rational voice interrupted.

Dummy, this isn't a date. What are you thinking? It doesn't matter if you wear your hair up, down, or side-ways—you are no match, you're not even on the same team as Isabel Chase. This is about Dad's cheating, not Connor's. Not that I think Connor would cheat, anyway.

I stepped closer to the mirror, analyzing my flaws. People told me I had a heart-shaped face, which I guess was good. I had nice lips, but I tried to keep them closed when I smiled because of my gap tooth. My hair was light brown in the summer and wavy (meaning it frizzed easily). It came an inch below my shoulders. My eyes were brown, kind of deep set, not like Frankenstein or anything. Some girls in my class were always being told they were pretty, but only a few people ever really ever told me that (my dead mom, my dead dad, and Beth). Mostly people would ask me why I looked so sad or worried or preoccupied. That was a question I got a lot. I assumed it was because I was so self-conscious of my smile and hardly ever smiled, but now I realized it was in my eyes.

Before I left, I knocked quietly at Beth's bedroom.

"Come in." Her voice was hoarse.

I opened the door a few inches. She was sitting on a chair by the window, her knees pulled to her chest. The lights were off. Dusk lit the room in a soft glow.

"Um, I just wanted to tell you I'm going to the movies with some friends."

Beth wiped her eyes with her sleeve. She cleared her throat before speaking. "Okay. Have fun. When will you be back?"

Normally she would have asked which friends. Then again, I rarely went out at all anymore. For all I knew, she was just relieved to have time alone to herself.

"Not late, because I'll be with Rebs," I lied. "You remember Rebs, right?"

Beth nodded.

Of course, Rebs was already off in the wilds of Vermont. Last summer, before Dad died, Rebs and I had both sworn we'd return to Norwich. But here's the funny thing: at the time, I'd been lying to Rebs; I was already gunning for a more college-oriented job. I'd told Dad as much. But I knew that Beth wouldn't have known about my plans unless Dad told her. I hadn't mentioned Rebs to Beth since I'd fallen off the earth after Dad's death.

So why did I lie just now? Was I hoping Beth would burst out with what she knew about me . . . some confidence Dad had shared about me, about my summer plans, and my lie to my friend? Was I hoping to prove that he trusted Beth with my confidences, to prove that he wouldn't have cheated on her? To pre-empt meeting Connor at all?

I hesitated in the doorway before taking a few steps into the dim room. Maybe because of the darkness, because we were both only silhouettes in this light, it was easier to lose the annoyed tone I always took with her. "Beth," I began.

"Midnight?" she asked.

"Yeah, around then. I'll be fine. Don't worry about me. I cleaned the kitchen."

She drew in a breath. "Thank you."

"And I have money. Just my cash and my bank card 'on my person.'"

At that, she almost smiled. It was the closest we had to a private joke: Beth always advised to keep some cash and my bank card separate from my wallet and purse, "on your person," just in case I lost them. And I always rolled my eyes.

"I'm sorry I got so upset," she said. "It's just so much change, dealing with Michael's death. And you'll be leaving for college soon. I feel . . ." She didn't finish.

"How do you feel?" I breathed.

She mustered a sad smile, her eyes red-rimmed and blood-shot. "Unhinged," she said. "That was the word I was going to use."

Unhinged. I knew exactly what she meant. My word was *adrift.* Dad was our anchor and now we were floating, lost. I realized for the first time that Beth might be upset I was leaving for college. Would she miss me? Even after how bratty and ungrateful I'd been? I couldn't bring myself to believe it. She'd be alone in this house. I'd lived every second of my life since Dad's death thinking that's what she wanted. Solitude. I was about to leave the room when I stopped myself.

"Beth," I said, turning back to her. "I know it's been weird between us, but I just want you to know . . ." My voice sped up so much all the words ran together. I was afraid if I didn't say it really quickly I would never have the courage to say it again. "I'm glad you didn't run off after Dad died."

I closed the door behind me and hurried down the stairs. I glanced at my phone: 8:47. I grabbed my canvas shoulder bag and ran through the kitchen. All that was left on the table was the pale pink peony in the vase.

Chapter Six

A crowd of high school kids and college students hung out on the steps in front of Amherst Cinema. I recognized a group of sophomores at my school and waved to them as I scanned the crowd for Connor. I hoped I wouldn't run into anyone else I knew tonight.

There.

Connor stood alone near the parking lot, half hidden in the shadows. He was talking on the phone, one hand pressed to his ear so he could block the noise. I could tell by the way he moved his hands that he was in the middle of a serious conversation. I assumed he was talking to his girlfriend, so I hung back, waiting. I put my earbuds in but didn't play anything. I admit it: I was trying to eavesdrop. But he was too far away and I couldn't hear anything.

I sat on a railing. It wasn't a dark night and the faint stars didn't really sparkle; they glowed behind the clouds. I had a strange kind of feeling I couldn't place. I was proud of myself for finally being at least sort of nice to Beth. She wasn't a terrible stepmom. She cared. It wasn't just a show for my dad. It made me feel less teenagery and more adult. What was the word I was looking for? The only thing that popped into my head at that moment was one that made me cringe—a totally Amhersty-hippie-New-Age-Wicca-type word that you see on bumper stickers all around here: EMPOWERED.

I couldn't even say "empowered" with any kind of straight face. But at that moment, I definitely felt a little more grown-up. Or like I was starting to grow up. Was I "in transition"? That's the New Age shrink with the amber necklace's favorite catch phrase. Maybe I was. If I could treat Beth like an actual human being, maybe I was breaking out of the teenage body-snatcher pod that hijacked me when I was thirteen and a half. FEELING GOOD ABOUT DOING GOOD, as the framed poster in her office proclaimed.

I glanced back toward Connor. He was still on the phone, leaning against the brick wall. I got up and walked toward him.

"Hey," I said quietly.

He looked up at me, covering the phone with his hand and mouthed, "Two minutes."

I nodded. As I watched, he turned his back on me and paced away so I would be out of earshot. I crossed my arms and leaned back against the wall. Now I was annoyed. He had told me to be here at 9:00. It was 9:20. If he'd known he'd be wrapped up in some kind of intense romantic drama with his tall, pretty, thin, smart, white-toothed girlfriend . . . Not that I was jealous. Irritated? He *was* doing me a favor after all.

Of course, I'd just assumed he'd help me break into Dad's old office to put my fears about philandering to rest. Connor hadn't said a thing other than to meet him. Maybe I was wrong.

I looked at my watch: 9:21. I'd give him five—no seven— more minutes before I . . . before I what? Got on my bike and went home? I liked to make dramatic threats I knew I wouldn't keep.

"Sorry," he called, hurrying over. "I'm really sorry. I know that was rude."

So now I would act like I barely even noticed.

"I was in the middle of . . ." He let his words trail off. He ran his fingers through his hair and winced as if he had a headache. He hadn't changed clothes; he'd just thrown on a dark grey zip-up hoodie sweatshirt, unzipped, so the world could see the braggy Stanford University logo.

But all at once he smiled.

I forgot how annoyed I was. I almost smiled back.

"So, um, I thought you wanted to try your hand at hacking," he said. He reached into his sweatshirt pocket, pulling out a ring of multi-lock copy-proof keys.

Now I did smile. "How'd you get those?"

"My dad's meeting ran late in Boston and he has another meeting in the morning so he's spending the night there. He left these keys in the car."

"Okay." I suddenly felt incredibly nervous. "Are we really going to do this?"

"Like I said before, I doubt you'll be able to get into your dad's emails. I mean . . ." Once again, he broke off in mid-sentence.

"What?" I pressed.

"Are you sure you want to know if he was having an affair?"

I shoved my hands in my pockets. I looked up at the sky. Good question. I was frightened. The idea of being caught by Harrison was frightening. But more frightening was the reason why neither Beth nor I had heard from him. If it wasn't an affair . . . what? But no, that was impossible—there had to be another explanation.

"Yes, I'm sure," I heard myself answer.

At night the bike path is lit by solar-powered lamps; they give off a milky glow, a row of small moons. I'd hardly ever ridden this late at night. I didn't want to pedal too fast, for fear of running into a deer or snake that might be walking along or crossing the path, even a bear. Yes, there were bears in these woods. Connor didn't seem to have the same worry. I struggled to keep up with him, the cool night air whipping across my face.

We passed only one other cyclist, exercising two black-and-white huskies who sped after him. The white of the dogs flashed by like ghosts: blurs of claws and fur and mirror-like eyes. I shivered as we pulled up toward the back entrance, where we'd snuck out.

The parking lot was empty, the windows dark. The only sounds were the purr from the highway in the distance and the drone of crickets all around us.

I saw then how we were going to get into the building—the fire escape. He must have returned to let the ladder down. I hoped no one had noticed; it was hidden beneath all the scaffolding.

"Can't we just go in the front door since you have the keys?" I whispered. I didn't want to climb up the four rusted, rickety flights again—especially not in the dark. For some reason I was more nervous about the fire escape collapsing than trespassing, which was an actual crime.

"Security cameras," he whispered back.

I nodded, feeling stupid. Of course there would be security cameras now, protecting the new computers and equipment. I checked my phone: 10:03. I turned the ringer off and shoved it back in my shoulder bag.

I stared up at the old brick building. Under the hazy pale moon, I could see the name of the paper mill, FORT RIVER MILL, peeling in faded red and yellow flakes. The windows on the top floor of the building were completely black, nothing reflecting in them, as though they'd been covered with dark paper.

Connor climbed first and I followed. We moved quickly and didn't speak. My knees felt wobbly and my palms moist against the cold iron railing. When we reached the third floor, he crawled through the window that had been left ajar. If there were cameras here, too, I couldn't see them among the jungle gym–like bars of the scaffolding. I stepped onto the window ledge. He held out his arms to me. I hesitated and our eyes caught. It may have only been for one or two seconds, but at the time it felt almost impossible to look away from him. The distance from the windowsill to the floor of the old factory building was maybe five feet. I could jump it, but he wasn't going to let me. I felt his hand on my waist as he lowered me down to the floor.

Connor pointed his flashlight on the creaky wooden floor

as we made our way down the hall toward my dad's office. Suddenly a bright white light glared in our eyes. We froze, statue-still. My heart raced and at the same time I felt freezing cold. *The alarm is going to sound.* I held my breath. Connor pointed to a corner of the ceiling where a rectangular, beige-colored box flashed a red light.

"It's just a light sensor," he said. I could hear the fear in his voice, like an echo. "It'll turn off in a few seconds."

We came to my dad's office door. Even mildly panicked, the poster of the Piri Reis map tacked to the wood once again gave me a painful stir. That map *was* Michael Barrett. It was everything he loved; it was the way he viewed the world. It was a funny thing; I don't remember anyone else even *mentioning* Piri Reis—not my mom, not Beth, not Harrison, not my teachers at school, though to hear Dad tell it, Piri Reis deserved to be as famous as Einstein or da Vinci. I could hear his voice, delighting in the wild rumors throughout the centuries: "*Some crackpots still believe Piri Reis was abducted by aliens and flown up in a spaceship. As if that's the only plausible explanation for the map's accuracy. How else could he have drawn the contours of the Americas? No cartographer back then could have possibly accounted for the curvature of the Earth, right? It's so ridiculous! But that's the thing about people. They'd rather believe in UFOs than the truth. He had a natural eye for space, for distances . . . just like you, Tanya.*"

"Are you okay?" Connor whispered.

I blinked. "Yeah." I nodded, trying to shut out the memory. "But, hey, Connor, did you ever find out if your dad came by our house this winter?"

His eyes softened. "Dad's in Boston, Tanya," he gently reminded me. "I haven't talked to him all day. Why do you ask?"

I jerked my head at the map. "My dad kept the actual lithograph of that map in the shed. It's this old—"

"The Piri Reis map," Connor interrupted. A concerned, puzzled smile played on his lips. "I know, Tanya. Remember? I probably spent more time total listening to your dad lecture me about that map than I spent in any class at Stanford this year." He began to tick off facts. "It was drawn in 1513, but how could it have been drawn in 1513? Nobody knew about the curvature of the Earth—"

"Enough," I interrupted, but I had to laugh. "Let's just get this over with."

Connor slid the key into the lock. It was one of those specially made nonduplicate-able keys, and for a moment I wondered if it would work. But there was a click, and the door swung open easily. We slipped out of the floodlit hallway, closing and locking the office behind us. The floodlights remained on outside. I kept staring at the line of light under my dad's office door, waiting for it to disappear.

We worked in the dark. Connor shined the flashlight on the computer keyboard. I turned it on and waited for the screen to appear. A black-and-white picture appeared as the screen saver: a young woman holding a newborn baby in a hospital bed. My mother and me. Connor stared over my shoulder. My eyes felt heavy just looking at the photo. I let out a sigh—I wasn't expecting this. Sometimes the reality of their deaths seemed so removed, and other times the weight of it fell on me, making it impossible to move.

I felt Connor's hand on my shoulder. I quickly typed in

the MapOut email account and logged in under my dad's name. Right away his email account appeared, asking for three passwords.

Three? Who has three passwords? Connor had told me he'd made it difficult, but this felt like paranoia.

"I have the first two," Connor said. "The hackers emailed them to my dad, to his personal account."

My hands hovered above the keyboard. I noticed they were shaking slightly.

172 Madeville Road. Connor spelled out the letters.

"The name of the street my mom grew up on," I said. What's the next one?"

"Your full name, all one word, and your birthday, month and day."

I couldn't help but smile. I typed in tanyabluebarrett2/18.

On-screen, the door opened and another password box appeared.

"This is where the hackers got stuck," Connor said. "Your dad put a time lock on it, so if you type in the wrong password, it automatically shuts the computer down for twenty-four hours."

I swallowed, sitting back in the chair. Now I felt pressure. There was another password he used sometimes, but it wasn't coming to me. My mother's name? Beth's name? My sweet and long-dead childhood cat, Bootsy? No. It had to be something with letters and numbers. My dad had often lectured me about Internet security, especially when I first started going online. He was afraid of some creepy cyberspace predator out there. A mixture of letters and numbers. His voice floated back from the past: *"Something that's meaningful only to you.*" He had told me not to use names of family members but he had used mine—so had he broken his own rule, again?

My mind was blank. Connor sat beside me picking at the cuticle around his thumbnail. I saw him doing this from the corner of my eye, and turned, looking at him. He had had this habit since he was a kid. I had a clear memory of us, sitting in my dad's outdoor shed right after his parents separated and his mother moved out. We were playing a game of checkers on a towel on the splintery floor. He was picking at the skin on his thumb so badly that he'd bled.

My head jolted up. I put my fingers on the keyboard. The poster in my dad's shed, the picture on his office door, the cartographer that nobody else seemed to know or care about. That was it, the other password: Piri Reis.

Nothing happened. Nothing opened but nothing closed. The computer didn't shut down. There was another part of the code. Letters and numbers. But what numbers? Maps were all numbers.

"Fifteen thirteen?" Connor whispered.

"The date the map was made," I heard myself whisper back. Of course. Why hadn't I thought of that? I hid a secret smile and shook my head, typing in the numbers. The screen unfolded, revealing a series of emails, and I felt a surge of relief. My eyes narrowed. The last was dated March 21. Five days before he died. I scrolled down the list. All were to and from C. Wright.

The name rang an instant bell. Cleo Wright: one of my dad's oldest friends. "The hippie with the horse farm," as Beth called her. She lived in New Mexico. Relief turned to suspicion. It couldn't be. Had Beth been right? Was he having an affair with some old flame he'd passed off as a friend?

I read the subject line of the last email aloud: "Alaska is an inkwell." I turned to Connor, who looked equally baffled. "What does that mean?"

He shook his head. I scrolled down to read the email before that one, sent from my dad.

Blackout Alaska. Stakes. 72 miles. 41 North. End.

I clicked the last email he received from her. It had never been opened.

Leave this alone and cease contact. Confirm receipt of this email.

There was no reply sent from my dad. Had he ever even received it?

"Wait, let me see this." Connor reached for the keyboard, typing in Alaska. He pressed the SEARCH button. Alaska appeared seventy-two times. Connor's face went pale as he frantically scanned the text.

"What is it?" I could see the pale blue light from the computer screen reflecting in his flitting eyes.

"I'm not sure yet. I overheard my dad talking about Alaska on the phone a couple nights ago. He was agitated. Not pissed . . . like, nervous. I'm not sure if he invested money in Alaska or what is going on."

A sound came from the hallway, a door closing.

I gripped Connor's arm, putting my finger over my lips.

We stared at each other. Silence. Had I imagined it? No. We both turned to see the dark strip beneath the door light up from the motion sensor. The office was dark, the door was locked, but there was no escape. I tiptoed to the window, peering out: nothing but a drop. Outside the office door, we heard footsteps and the muffled sound of voices. Lots of them. They drew closer, too many footsteps to count, until they seemed to be right outside the door.

My heart thumped wildly in my chest. But they kept moving.

Connor signaled to me to stay and put his ear against the door, listening. My mind raced through all kinds of nightmare scenarios of having to explain our break-in to Beth, to Harrison. I'd be fired, of course. Fired for trying to prove or disprove my dead father had been having an affair.

The last thing I heard were their footsteps walking upstairs to the floor above us.

"We better get out of here," Connor whispered.

My pulse was still racing. Before I shut down the computer, I clicked on the emails from Cleo, sending them to myself. Then I turned the computer off. The office went dark. We quickly locked the door behind us and kept low, avoiding the motion sensor, as we made our way down the hallway—out the window to the back fire escape. The night air had grown cooler. The building was dark except for two windows from the floor above us. I didn't feel safe. I don't know what I felt. Confused. Exhausted. Angry.

For some reason, Connor didn't climb down the fire escape; he climbed up, toward the lighted windows and the soft voices.

I glared at him. Did he want to get caught? But at the same time I was curious. Who else would be here so late at night? I found myself creeping up beside Connor, squinting through the bottom of the windowpane.

A group of five men and three women were looking at diagrams on a large computer screen. Grown-ups, in suits. It could have been a business meeting anywhere in the world. There was nothing strange about the scene at all, except for the hour. That, and I didn't recognize any of the participants as MapOut employees. The only person I recognized was Harrison, Connor's dad.

"I thought your dad was in Boston," I whispered, turning to him.

Connor's eyes were focused. "So did I."

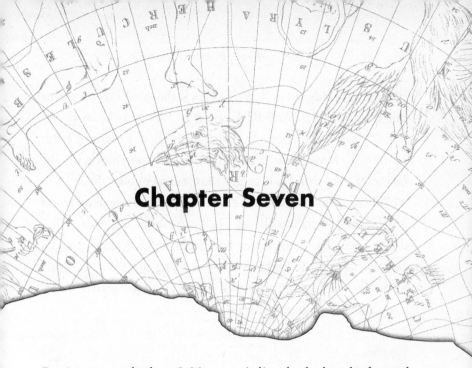

Chapter Seven

Rao's was packed at 8:30 A.M. A line had already formed out the door and all the tables were taken. Music from the Amherst College radio station sounded from the speakers and the spaced-out sounding DJ's voice came through reciting a public service announcement. My eyes felt dry and achy from only an hour or two of sleep.

I kept turning to the door every five seconds, waiting for Connor to arrive.

He was late.

Last night, after spotting Connor's dad, we'd bolted back down the fire escape. Connor needed to get home. He was nervous, panicky, muttering about how he needed to put the office keys back in the hidden compartment under the front seat of Harrison's car before his dad got back and noticed they were gone.

I ordered a latte and a toasted poppy seed bagel with cream cheese and slumped down at the one empty spot at the communal table. I tried not to check the time on my phone but couldn't stop. At 9:02 I began to feel panicky, too. My hands shook as I lifted the coffee to my lips. I realized I was hungry. I chewed my bagel, listening to the chatter of the radio DJ. Anything was better than awful music.

Where was he? Maybe he had overslept? Forgotten to set his alarm? Somehow being the overachiever he was, that didn't seem like something he would do. I double-checked our texts from the night before—starting at 1:55 A.M.—just to make sure I hadn't missed something, that I wasn't losing my mind or imagining things.

Connor
Dad's still not home.

Tanya
Maybe it was some kind of emergency meeting.

Connor
Called his hotel in Boston—he never checked out. Do not disturb on his room.

Tanya
Strange. I can barely sleep.

Connor
Me too.

Tanya
I thought you hated texting. ☺

Connor
I do. This is torture. What do those emails say?

Tanya
Can't open them. They show as scrambled code on my computer. Obv. encrypted—duh. Tried emailing Cleo 10 X. All returned, undeliverable. Haven't found Cleo's number yet. I know she lived in Elk, New Mexico.

Connor
Same problem here. Can't get into my dad's emails. He put a double password on too. Searched Alaska on his computer. All that came up was a map of Alaska.

Tanya
Maybe Alaska is a code between my dad and Cleo? A meeting place? A hotel?

Connor
Heard my dad mention it too, remember? Am searching through old phone bills for numbers in the 907 area code. That's Alaska by the way.

Tanya
Doing the exact same thing over here.

Connor
Paper phone bills date back two years ago but nothing in 907 code. His bills are online now—can't access but pretty sure my dad wasn't in contact with Cleo. I'm going to ask Dad about it when he gets home.

Tanya

What if he loses it again? Says it's none of your business.

Connor

Btw he gave me 4% ownership. I have a right to know what's going on.

Tanya

Found Dad's old phone and charger. I kept telling him he had to recycle it but he never did. Guess whose number is on it?

Connor

Cleo's?

Tanya

Yep. I'm going to call in the AM. She'll be able to answer our questions.

Connor

I want to be there when you call. Meet me at Rao's 8:30 AM. Try to get some sleep.

Tanya.
Ok. Good night.

Connor

Sleep tight.

• • •

When that last text came, I put the phone down on my bed-side table and set the alarm for 7:40 A.M. I'd just turned off the lamp and sunk my head down on the pillow when I heard the cricket-chirp sound of another text.

Connor
Hey... ok you know I'm not the best texter in the world and it's not my favorite way of communicating but I just need to tell you something.

Tanya
What is it?

The phone rang as I stared at it, waiting for him to answer my text.

"Connor?"

"Hi. I'm sorry. I know it's late."

"That's okay. What is it? Did you find something?"

"No. I'm not calling about that." He drew an audible breath. I pressed the phone to my ear. We hadn't spoken on the phone since we were kids. I remembered having quick and stilted conversations with him from my pink princess phone in my room. Mostly what I remembered was tangling the cord around my finger over and over again until it got stuck, untangle-able. I was still wondering why he had to *call*. I clenched the pillow in my hand, listening.

"I just wanted to tell you in person, not in text, that it was really good to see you today. I mean . . ." He sounded flustered, his words rushing together. "I mean better than good. To spend time with you."

I held my breath. Did he really just say that? Or had I misheard him?

"Tanya? You there?"

"Yeah." My voice sounded weak, hollow. The dark room swam around me. I pressed the phone against my cheek and ear. I felt frozen, waiting to unfreeze.

"Okay, well, I guess I'll see you tomorrow at Rao's?" he finished.

I didn't speak. *Be brave*, I thought. *Tell him.*

"Good night," he said softly.

"Connor, wait." I imagined I was shouting but my voice was just a whisper.

"Yeah?"

"Um." I inhaled. "I wanted to say . . . I also missed you . . ." Now that I had started telling him this I didn't know how to end it. I was aware I might be saying too much but at the same time I thought I had to explain what I meant in a way that would make it seem . . . casual. "I mean because we were friends when we were kids and our parents were friends. You knew my mom and my dad. I guess I just miss everything about that time. You know?"

Thank God he couldn't see my agonized, contorted expression. Thank God he hadn't FaceTimed me. Why did saying the truth feel so awkward and crazy?

"I do know," he said, jumping in just before I plummeted.

"You do?"

"Yeah. Remember I told you I wanted to work for Habit for Humanity?"

"Yeah?"

"My dad was really pressuring me to work for him at

MapOut, he kept using the term 'family business' to guilt me into it. When he mentioned you were working there, too . . . I guess it was part of the reason I said yes. A big part. The only part, really."

I smiled, blinking rapidly in the darkness.

"That's all," he said, and then he was gone.

Connor had hung up at 2:47. I looked up from my phone into the crowded café, once again searching for him. Maybe he was still asleep. Boys slept a lot, like they could sleep all day. After our phone call *I* could barely sleep. I'd replayed the conversation about one thousand and fifty-seven times in my head. I wondered if he had, too?

It was 9:20. I imagined him asleep in bed, his face in the pillow, the sheet rumpled around him. I decided to send one more text. Maybe he was sick of the phone and would just show up. Or his phone was dead and he couldn't find a charger. The possibilities were endless. I envisioned a bike crash, the gravel cutting into his hands and face. My thumb twitched over the SEND button, and I forced myself to press it.

Hey I'm still here. At common table in the back.

I put the phone down. I closed my eyes, resting them in the palms of my hands. When I open them, I told myself, he would either be here or there would be a text from him. If I didn't leave in the next five minutes I would be late for work. I stood up, carrying the empty cup to the plastic bin.

Outside, the sun stung my eyes. I wondered if I should call Cleo, but I didn't want to do it alone. As I walked to my bike, I rehearsed what I would say to her in my head. All versions of the story sounded crazy and seriously paranoid. I hadn't seen her in years and now I was going to call out of the blue and say, "Hey, it's Tanya. What's up? I hacked into my dad's personal emails and I'm wondering if you were having an affair with him? And what's the deal with Alaska?"

Last night, when I was planning to make the call, all my thoughts felt clear, logical—but now standing in the bright sunlight I felt something I'd never felt before, a confusion I couldn't name. But secretly I imagined that it was what someone like Beth must feel if she were lost. Someone with no direction, stuck without a map. So maybe I could name it "unhinged."

I arrived at MapOut at 10:15. The receptionist with the short black hair and powder-pale skin was sipping a can of Diet Coke. She looked up at me, the can of soda in her hand as she chewed on the straw.

I kind of mouthed the word *morning* as I hurried past.

"Hey there," she called out. Before I even turned around, I heard the sound of her soda can against the desk. She stared intently at the large computer screen on her desk.

"I don't think we've formally met yet," she said. She had a low voice, not soft, just low and quick.

"I'm Tanya Barrett. I'm just working for the summer."

"I know. I remember your dad. I'm Alison."

"Nice to meet you." I smiled back at her. "Do you know if Connor is here yet?" I felt awkward asking, like maybe she would think I had a crush on him or something, so I quickly added. "He was supposed to show me how to use the Track program."

She glanced at her screen, her eyes scrolling down what looked like a series of numbers.

"Nope. Not yet." She smiled a smile that froze in place for at least three seconds or more.

"Okay." I bit my top lip. "Um, is Harrison in yet?"

"Nope. He's in Boston. He should be back this afternoon." She glanced back at her screen, her eyes following the scroll of numbers. "And your phone number is?"

"My phone number?"

"Updating contact info."

I told her my number.

"Okay." She typed in the number. "And you still live at 48 Lincoln Road, Amherst?"

"Yes."

"Okay," she said without looking away from the screen. "We're good."

One of the top ten most annoying expressions: *we're good*. I walked past her and into the cavernous office space. Most of the employees had already arrived. The morning sun cast slanted rectangles of light across the wooden floors. All the white cubicles were full of the scruffy college types, inputting data, the keyboards making soft clicking sounds that filled the room.

The kitchen was empty. The coffee pot only had a drop of coffee left. I checked my phone again. Nothing. I poured the dregs of the coffee into my cup and walked to my cubicle. The guy working next to me sort of nodded a brief hello. He had his earbuds in and I could hear the tinny sound of music coming through. The pile of data reports I hadn't finished yesterday sat beside me. I wanted to scream at it.

I picked up a page from the pile of data info, but could barely focus. At this point I was a combination of mostly worried, annoyed, impatient, and confused. What time was it in New Mexico? Should I just go ahead and phone Cleo without him? It was only 10:32 A.M.

Calm down, I thought. *He'll be here soon.*

At 11:57 I broke my vow of not checking my phone until 12:30. I pressed SLEEP, and the computer screen went black and announced to the three walls of my cubicle that I was taking an early lunch break. I picked up my knapsack, went to the newly renovated toilets, and splashed handfuls of cold water on my face and the back of my neck. My eyes looked puffy and sort of bloodshot. If anyone saw me they would probably think I was a stoner. Of course, half the people who worked here were probably stoners. I smoothed my hair with my hands and pulled it back into a ponytail.

I can get away with taking my lunch break now.

I took the keys to my bike lock from my knapsack and retrieved the buried phone. As I neared Harrison's office, I could see it was still empty. The receptionist was talking into her phone headset. I tried to hurry out without her noticing. But just as I was about to walk through the front door out into the sunshine, she looked up from her computer screen.

"Lunch break?" she asked, her eyes popping up.

"Yep."

"You get forty-five minutes."

"Yep. I know."

"All good." Her eyes flashed back to the screen. The quickness and intensity of her typing was more like a concert pianist than an office assistant. No wonder Dad and Harrison had hired her.

Outside, the bright sun glared against the concrete parking lot. I got on my bike and rode down the bike path half a mile away to Silvia's Polish Café, a small place right off the bike trail next to Trailside Ice Cream and the River Bend Dance School. I left my bike on the crowded bike rack. Now I thought I could turn my phone on. I watched anxiously as the screen lit up. I was sure Connor would have gotten back to me by now—I hadn't checked my phone in one long hour and thirty-five minutes.

There were two new voice mails.

No texts.

The first one was from Beth.

"Hey there." (*Hey there* was her way of trying to sound cool and casual even when she was checking up on me.) "You must have gotten back late last night. I didn't see you this morning. Just checking in to see if you're okay. Will you be in for dinner tonight? I . . . anyway, have a good day at work. See you later."

The next voice mail was from an 802 number I didn't recognize right away. The only thing I knew was that it was from Vermont.

"Tanya! Hon!" yelled Rebs.

My heart squeezed thinking of her at the Norwich summer camp. I imagined her . . . swimming, eating in the cafeteria, teaching arts and crafts in the rec hall—where the air smelled of citronella bug spray and sun block, and the floor was always damp from the kids trekking in with wet bathing suits from the lake.

"We barely have cell service up here! It's like *Little House on the Prairie*. I have to walk to the 'town' post office to get any cell reception. That's why you haven't heard from me, like, every single day. We're having a counselor party Friday night we seriously want you to come. Call Blaney, she's driving up with some of her friends from Smith. You've got to come. Luv ya, mean it."

I nodded as I hung up, forgetting that she couldn't see me. Blaney was Rebs's older sister. I would call Blaney as soon as I figured out why the hell Connor hadn't shown up today at MapOut. Actually, scratch that: I would call Cleo first, with or without Connor. He still had not returned my last pathetic text and now I was in a shame spiral, regretting I'd ever sent it. Obviously I had a semi crush on him. Maybe he'd lost his phone? Maybe he just wasn't texting me back. It sucked, but sometimes you have to be a realist.

I'd copied Cleo's phone number from my dad's old phone into mine the night before. It was a New Mexico area code: 725.

I took a deep breath. I don't know why I was so nervous exactly. This was one of my dad's oldest friends. True, I hadn't seen Cleo since she came to Amherst four years ago. She was tall and thin with long, wavy, sun-bleached hair. She reminded me of the models in the Sundance Catalog my mom used to order clothes from. Plus, she loved horses and was a great equestrian—a nature girl, but also kind of tough talking. She had light brown skin and freckles. I remembered that when we went out to dinner, she always ordered a double bourbon on the rocks. It had never occurred to me that my dad would have an affair with Cleo for the simple reason that Cleo never showed any interest in him. My dad was fine looking, but when I pictured Cleo with a guy, it was George Clooney.

Now that I thought about it, Cleo had never mentioned men at all, nor had Dad ever mentioned a man in her life.

I dialed the number and pressed my phone to my ear, counting the rings. My phone felt hot. Three rings, then a woman's voice picked up.

"Hello?" It was Cleo, no question.

"Cleo? It's Tanya, Michael's daughter." There was a pause on the other end. For a moment I thought we'd been disconnected. "It's Tanya," I repeated. "Michael Barrett's daughter. Um, I'm calling because—"

"Please don't call this number again."

"What? Cleo?"

She had already hung the phone up.

I felt as if I were falling. I pressed the number again, the phone spinning in my clammy hand. Not even a single ring. The call wouldn't go through. She had blocked it.

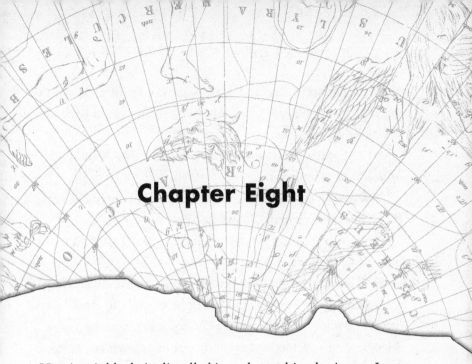

Chapter Eight

Harrison's black Audi pulled into the parking lot just as I was locking up my bike.

I wondered if Connor was in the car. I couldn't see anything through the shaded windows. It was 1:04 P.M. Was Harrison returning from home or had he driven back to Boston after his late-night meeting at MapOut? Would he have seen Connor? Did he know where he was? I lingered, taking my time clipping my helmet to the handlebars and retying my shoe. Waiting for Harrison to get out of his car. But the car doors remained closed, the engine continued to run, the dark windows sealed. The sun reflected off the black hood. He was sitting in his air-conditioned car with the windows rolled up, talking on his phone.

After a few minutes I gave up and walked into the MapOut office. The cool, overly air-conditioned air reminded me of being on an airplane. I wished I could go back outside. It was a beautiful day, not too hot or humid. My dad was big into conservation and unless it was boiling he would never turn on the AC. On a day like this he would have just opened the windows.

1:12. I knew the time because Alison, the receptionist, announced as much.

"We really try to keep the lunch break to forty-five minutes," she commented. "It's policy."

"I was only gone an extra eight minutes." I tried to make light of it, to smile at her.

She continued to look at her computer screen. "It's policy," she repeated. "If everyone added eight minutes to their lunch break it would equal X number of hours of lost work over time." All of a sudden she looked up with a smile and winked at me.

I stared at her. There was no way I could respond to a wink even if I wanted to win this argument. Without another word I made my way back to my desk. The pile of input data next to my computer looked as though it had doubled in height since I was last at my cubby an hour ago. At first I thought it was my imagination. Then I saw the yellow Post-it: *Harrison needs these finished by end of day. Thanks! Alison.* She had signed it with a smiley face.

Was Harrison kidding about these pages? Even if I was on schedule with yesterday's work, there was no way I could realistically finish by the end of the day. I pulled her Post-it off the pile and crumpled it angrily in my hand.

A text came through on my phone. I immediately checked, expecting a response from Connor. It was from Rebs.

Hi T! Blaney driving up tonight @ 9. Hitch a ride with her! Tote desp. for you to come!

Staring at the pile of work on my desk, I regretted that

I'd ever applied for this job in the first place. I wished I was with everyone else at Camp Norwich lifeguarding on the lake. I wished I'd never seen Connor again, never seen his dad, never second-guessed Beth or my own father.

Yes I want to come! I frantically typed back. Give Blaney my # and tell her I'll pitch in for gas and beer!

I smiled as I waited for Rebs to reply. I felt as if a weight had been flung from my shoulders. Here I was, just a normal girl, joking around with a friend, on her way up to party for the weekend. I could almost pretend it was true. I could make it true. I *would*. I stole a quick glance around the office. The front desk was empty. Alison wasn't there. A pen lay at an angle over a white pad of paper with the MapOut logo printed across the top. The ever-present can of Diet Coke sat beside the keyboard.

I was about to leave when the doors of Harrison's office opened. I hesitated. Was it guilt? But why would I feel guilty? He was the one who'd lied about his whereabouts last night. No . . . I froze because I hoped I'd see Connor.

Alison stepped out. The doors swung shut behind her.

"Can I help you?" She adjusted her rectangular blacked-rimmed eyeglasses and smoothed her skirt as she sat down in her swivel chair.

I suddenly realized I'd been staring at her. I was about to explain that there was no way I could finish the pile she had left for me, when the doors opened again. Harrison walked out of his office.

"Tanya." He smiled, opening his arms to me. This was the way he'd always greeted me, with a hug. "Do you have a minute?"

I shrugged. "Sure."

He looked surprisingly fresh-faced, clean shaven—in a pale blue button-down and jeans. I could still see the crisp lines from where the shirt had been pressed. I could smell the familiar mint-spice scent of his aftershave that lingered around him. It reminded me of my dad; he used the same brand. It always had the effect of making me want to take one step closer to him.

I followed him into his office: a bright corner room lined with ceiling-to-floor windows. A modern brown leather sofa sat against the wall, across from his stainless-steel desk, with two chairs facing from the other side. In the other corner was an old video arcade game from the '80s. PAC-MAN.

"Does that actually work?" I asked, dazzled by the whole setup. In comparison, my dad's office was like the supply cupboard. I instantly regretted having opened my mouth. Harrison had no idea I'd been in my dad's office.

"Have a seat, Tanya." He gestured to one of the chairs in front of his desk.

He gripped the arms of his chair as he sat down. His smile was gone. He leaned back and closed his eyes for a moment. When he opened them again, his expression was even graver. "You know your father made me your legal guardian."

I blinked at him. Those were the last words I was expecting to hear. I'd always assumed Beth was my legal guardian. She was the one who dealt with feeding me, housing me, providing me with spending money. We may not have communicated, but she was *there*. I shrugged again, not sure how to answer.

"It's a responsibility I take very seriously. You also know I love and care about you deeply. In fact, I think of you as my own daughter. My second child. So I need you to be honest with me. Understood?"

In the bright light from his office, I could see the large dark circles beneath his eyes. I could also see he had tried to disguise them with powder or cover-up. It looked normal from a distance but in this light, up close, the streaks were visible. This all felt very wrong, all of a sudden, his putting me on the spot. He'd lied to his own son about where he was. What the hell was he trying to hide, anyway?

"I have a few questions to ask you," he continued. "All I want from you is the truth." He leaned forward. "Can you promise me that, Tanya?"

"Okay." My throat felt thick, heavy.

"What time did you leave work yesterday?"

I took a deep breath and let it out slowly. No need to panic. Okay. So someone had ratted on us. (And I already had a prime suspect: Alison.) I was being busted for sneaking out early. That was fine. I could handle this.

"Sorry. Yeah. I left early. It was a really nice day and—"

He held his hand up to stop me. "What time did you return to MapOut?"

"Um . . . this morning. I'm not exactly sure . . . like around ten."

His eyes met mine, holding them. "The truth, please." His voice was calm but I could tell he was upset. He clenched the arms of his stainless-steel chair as he waited for an answer.

I repeated my first answer. "Around ten A.M."

Harrison shook his head. "You and Connor came back to MapOut at 10:42 last night and you left at 11:56."

I froze. I felt a queasy rush as the color drained from my

face. We'd been caught. Who had seen us? When did they see us? If they knew when we came and left, obviously they were spying on us the whole time. Why hadn't they confronted us?

I blinked several times, unable to speak. He turned the large computer screen on his desk to face me. On it was a list of ten-digit numbers. Telephone numbers. All the employee telephone numbers all with times and dates next to them.

"You're clocking your employees by their phones?" I gasped.

His features softened. "That's right. That's why lying won't do you—"

"Is that actually legal?" I interrupted.

"Is the punch card legal?" Harrison asked, but he no longer sounded upset. A smile flickered across his face. "Look, Tanya, you're not in trouble. But I want you to know that I can't help you unless we're honest with each other."

I tried to smile back, to appease him somehow, but I felt as if I were suffocating. My dad would never have allowed something like this. It was creepy. Why was Harrison so paranoid about his employees' comings and goings? But then it hit me: he really *did* have something to hide. There was no other explanation.

"Where's Connor?" I asked.

Harrison stood and turned to the window, gazing out at the parking lot, the bright green leaves casting shadows over his face in the summer breeze. "I need to trust my employees. What you and Connor did was illegal. I know you were trying to hack into your dad's computer. Connor already told me."

I shook my head. This was wrong. I had already been caught in a lie. Maybe this was a trick question. Did he already know we'd been successful? How much had Connor told him, if anything? No. No way. I couldn't believe he'd tell his father a word, not after he'd made me swear to keep silent. It was best to tell the truth as far as I possibly could. I tried to laugh it off, but the sound died in my throat. "Well, yeah, see Beth thought my dad was having an affair with his old friend Cleo. You remember her?"

"And what did you find out?" Harrison asked, his back still turned to me. "Was he having an affair?"

I held my breath. If he could track people from their phones it was possible—unlikely but possible—he might have some way of reading texts. Had he read the texts I'd sent Connor? I should have been smarter than to be so explicit. I wracked my brain, trying to remember exactly what I'd written. There was a chance that Harrison didn't know the whole truth.

Harrison shoved his hands in his coat pockets and turned around. "You are aware that breaking and entering is a serious crime—as is hacking. As owner of the company I would owe it to my shareholders and investors to prosecute you and Connor. I would be legally and ethically obliged to do so."

"But I didn't find anything out!" I practically shouted. "I couldn't get past the third password." So much for telling the truth. On the other hand, he'd just told me that I had nothing to be scared of, and now he was threatening to file criminal charges? That would put an end to my college applications, to any future jobs. I felt that invisible weight I'd just shed talking to Rebs clamp down on me, forcing me through the seat, through the floor, under the earth. Who would help me? I didn't have a mother or father. Would I need a lawyer? Would I go to jail? How serious was this? What had I done?

I wasn't really a crier. I mean, I did cry, but I usually held it in until I was alone somewhere. Maybe it was the lack of sleep, or the magnitude of what he was saying, but I didn't have any strength left in me. Wetness stung my eyes. I looked up at the ceiling to keep the tears from falling, but it was hopeless. This was a different kind of crying. I wasn't sad or upset; I was afraid.

"Tanya, sweetheart." I felt Harrison's hand on my shoulder.

Everything had gone wrong today. And all because of a stupid bet with Connor yesterday afternoon. But no, that was unfair—to both of us. I wished I had never snuck out with him, wished I'd never trusted a word that had come out of his mouth. I forced myself to look up at Harrison.

"Like I said before, I care about you like my own child," he said. "So I'm not going to tell the police. I'll give you a second chance. But you need to make up for the hours you skipped out with Connor yesterday. I'd like you to be part of MapOut's future. I know your dad would have wanted that, too."

He reached across his desk and handed me a tissue. I couldn't bring myself to thank him. "You have a talent," he went on. "You always have. Remember the bird's-eye view drawing you made of your house and yard? Of your dad's work shed? All the measurements were exact and you were barely out of kindergarten."

I wiped my eyes with the tissues. He had pretended he was going to prosecute me—but why? To scare me? To make me cry? To show that he had much more power than me?

"You're a paid employee like everyone else. Make up the hours and we can put this behind us." He sat back behind his desk and swung his screen around so it was facing him again. "You need guidance, Tanya, you have to know what you did was wrong. Not only wrong but against the law. I've been much easier on you than I have on Connor."

"Where *is* Connor?" I asked again. My voice was scratchy but clear.

"En route to California. He hopped on an early flight on a whim. He missed his girlfriend. I'm still annoyed, but I respect his decisions. Besides, I'd like to open an office out there, and I've tasked him with finding MapOut a new office space."

For a second, I thought I misunderstood. "When you say en route . . . ?" I couldn't finish my own question.

"He's gone back to California. He missed his girlfriend." Harrison said. He dug in his pants pocket for his cell phone and started scrolling through it.

Gone. I wanted to get up, to run from the office, but I felt stuck to the chair. Time seemed to stand still. Connor didn't even say goodbye. He'd told me he'd come back to be with me. That was the *last thing* he'd said. It didn't matter how much he hated phones; he wasn't that much of a creep. I knew it. It made absolutely no sense. Unless . . .

Unless things were better with his girlfriend than he'd hinted; unless he didn't want to jeopardize his future by breaking into his dad's office with a sort of regular-looking girl from his childhood; unless he was embarrassed by the confession he'd made and wished he could take it back.

"Do we have an understanding, Tanya?" Harrison asked.

He didn't bother looking up from his phone. "You probably should get back to work."

I nodded mutely and left before any more tears could come.

At my cubicle I counted the pages. I felt numb. Maybe I could work hard, forget Connor, finish this project, and save some face here. Refocus on doing well and getting into a good college. I could be done by 8:00 P.M. After that: escape. From everything. I needed to see my friends. To get away from all this, even just for two days. But I couldn't stop thinking about Connor. Maybe he was on the plane now. Maybe he would call or text me when he landed. Maybe he would apologize for being a liar and a coward.

Or maybe I'd never hear from him again.

At 5:00, the construction workers started leaving. I was almost halfway through the pile of data entry. The building settled into a strange kind of quiet. I went to the kitchen, poured myself a large coffee and added cream. I didn't even want it but my energy was sinking.

I stirred the coffee and looked out the window, at the parking lot below. I saw Harrison, his phone pinned to his ear, walking quickly to his car. I saw the three brothers from MIT riding away on their bikes. The sun was setting behind the trees, casting long shadows across the ground. Back at my desk I forced myself to work. I'd completed three-fourths of the pile but I was struggling to keep my concentration.

My phone pinged next to me. It was Blaney, Rebs's sister.

Blaney
Hey, where are u?

Tanya
At MapOut. I have to work late (long story). I should be done by
8:30 maybe a little longer.

Blaney
K. I'll pick you up at work. It's the warehouse building on Essex
St. right?

Tanya
Yep.

Blaney
@ 9 just to be safe.

Tanya
Thx.

I knew I had to call Beth or she would seriously worry. I dialed
Beth's number.

She picked up on the first ring. "Tanya? Are you okay?"

"Yeah, I—"

"It's late."

"I know. I'm . . . sorry. I just got swamped with work. I
lost track of the time."

There was a pause. She cleared her throat. "I didn't see
you this morning. You must have left early."

"Yeah. Lots of work, like I said. Um . . . but I'm calling to
let you know I'm going to spend the weekend with Rebs and
her sister at Camp Norwich They're having a big counselor-
reunion party-type thing. Blaney's picking me up here after
work so I won't be home."

Another pause.

"Hello?" I said.

"Oh, okay, so when will you be back?"

"Sunday."

"Sunday," Beth echoed. She sounded disappointed. It honestly made me depressed hearing this in her voice. "Did you bring an overnight bag?"

"No. I'll just wear Rebs's clothes."

"What about a toothbrush?"

I rolled my eyes. "I'll buy one . . . I better go now."

"Call me if you need a ride back—"

"Okay, thanks. Bye." I clicked off.

I stared back at the computer screen. My eyes were so fatigued the words were literally swimming. I struggled through a few more pages when I heard footsteps. It was Alison, walking quickly toward me, the heels of her shoes clicking against the wood floor. Her car keys jangled in her hand.

"I'm leaving. The lights will go off automatically when you leave. Smart Sensors. And just close the door behind you; it self-locks."

"Okay."

She flashed a brittle smile. "Looks like you've made some progress," she said, peering over my shoulder.

"Yep."

"See ya Monday." She waved and hurried away, the click of her heels echoing in the large room.

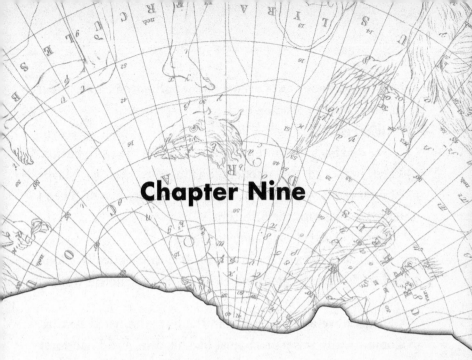

Chapter Nine

I got Connor's text at 8:20 P.M.

Sorry I didn't get a chance to say bye in person. Going back to California was a last-minute decision. MapOut needs a West Coast office space and they needed me to find it. I might not be exactly where I want to be but I'll keep looking. Your dad was an inspiration to me the way Perry Reese was to him. I know you understand. Hope the rest of your summer goes well.

I blinked at it.

I read it three more times. My stomach churned. For a second I was worried I might vomit. My eyes flashed to "Perry Reese." He hadn't bothered to fix the AutoCorrect. Either way, the unspoken message was clear: he didn't give a shit.

I bit my bottom lip so hard it hurt. I tried to stop the tears but I couldn't help it. I felt achy sick. Just last night I'd been so happy we had become or were becoming friends again.

Now he was gone. Not even a phone call, just a careless text that he couldn't even be bothered to spell check.

It's spelled Piri Reis, idiot.

I texted back. My forefinger hovered over the SEND button. Then I noticed my phone didn't auto-correct it. Maybe Connor really was an idiot, I tried to convince myself. Then I reread the text for the fifth time.

Hope the rest of your summer goes well.

That was the worst line of all. It meant basically "don't call me." God, I hated him. I stared at the cubicle walls. I really hated him.

A goodbye-forever text from the boy who hated texting. Connor really was a creep, just like his dad. And I had forty more minutes to stew about it. Forty minutes till Blaney rescued me from this place. I snapped up the phone and punched at the screen.

Thanks. Have a good summer too.

That sounded cold, like him, like his father. Tears welled in my eyes again but this time I fought them back. My finger lingered over the SEND button. Then I touched SEND.

"Shit."

I shouldn't have given him the satisfaction of a reply. I slammed the phone down. I felt so stupid. So completely idiotic. I thought we were close in a way nobody else could understand. I thought maybe we would even be closer. I wanted to scream, to smash the phone. But there was no point. He wouldn't hear me, anyway.

I couldn't concentrate or sit in front of the computer for one more second. I was done, even though I hadn't finished. I was done, as in spent: done with this place, done with this underpaid internship. The data could wait forever.

I pushed my chair back and paced around the office. Eventually I ended up by the large windows overlooking the empty parking lot. I felt tears burn in my eyes and tilted my head toward the ceiling, keeping them from rolling down my cheeks. I should know by now never to get my hopes up. Never to expect anything from anyone.

A car was pulling up in the driveway. Was Blaney early? I hoped so. I didn't see headlights, but there was definitely a purr of an idling engine nearby. Was that a Prius? Weren't they quieter? I held my phone as I made my way toward the bathrooms at the back of the building. After a splash of cold water on my face, I pulled my hair back. The bathroom lights flickered above like they do sometimes in a lightning storm. Then they went out. I walked to the door, hoping the sensor would restart them. Nothing. It was pitch black in the bathrooms.

My first thought was the janitor had turned off the lights thinking it was empty. But what about the light sensors?

"Hello?" I called. I felt my way to the bathroom door.

The lights were out in the whole office. The drone of a car engine came through the open window as I hurried back to my desk. Blaney was here. I picked up my bag, making my way into the stairwell. The sound of ascending footsteps echoed from below.

"Blaney?" I called.

Nobody answered.

"Blaney . . ."

My voice was a hollow whisper, barely passing my lips. I

stood in the darkness at the top of the stairs. It was like that moment in a dream when you try to run but you can't move. The sound of footsteps raced up the stairs. But nobody called out.

I turned from the double doors, pushed them closed, and fumbled for a way to lock them. No lock. Would the light sensors catch me? Had they been disabled, too? Probably. Whoever was coming turned off the main power to the building. The pale light from the moon cast long squares of light along the old warehouse floors. I could hear the faint words of a song coming from outside. I ran to the window. Blaney's Prius was there below, the windows rolled down.

The glow of her cell phone reflected off the front window. She was waiting for me. I felt my pockets. Where was my phone? Shit. I'd left it on my desk in a panic. I glanced across the room. My desk was on the other side of the building. I contemplated making a dash for it when the doors opened.

I stepped back from the window, pressing my back against the wall. I didn't know if I should run or stay still and hide in the shadows. From the corner of my eye I could see out the window to Blaney's car, its headlights shining on the gravel drive, the end of the song fading. *Don't leave. Don't leave.* Three figures crossed the room. One, a woman—I could tell by the shape of her body and hair—the other two, men.

They were silent, making their way with what seemed like preplanned precision from cubicle to cubicle. The fine white beam of a flashlight swept every square inch. I slid down against the wall, keeping myself as small as possible.

They divided themselves, the woman and one of the men

working toward the back of the room. One beam became three.

I slunk down farther, holding my breath. The tiny sound of a bird's whistle—my ringtone—chirped from my cell phone. *Oh God*. Blaney. She was right outside sitting in her car waiting for me, probably texting, Where are you??

The beams froze then converged, bouncing and disappearing as the three shadows hurried toward my cubicle. I heard the woman's voice but couldn't hear what she was saying. She had my phone. I couldn't hide much longer. They were as about far as they would get—43 feet away, I knew—with no direct path to my hiding place.

I crawled toward the heavy exit doors. There was a bar lock, so there was no way the flashlight people wouldn't hear me. But I had a plan: to jump out the fire escape Connor and I had used. I held my breath and sprinted the last ten feet. The doors pushed open with a clang. Their voices rose. I couldn't see anything in the hallway. Of course: they had cut the electricity. I felt along the walls with my hands. Blindness was not part of my plan. I ran with my arms stretched out in front of me.

There was a second fire door at the end of the hallway, exactly sixty feet from the first, which led to an inner stairwell and the exterior fire escape. The sound of the banging doors echoed behind me, followed by footsteps. They were here with me in this hall. I bolted ahead, counting my steps, careful to maintain three feet between each one. It was one thing to judge distance; it was another to control it. Running in the dark felt like walking on thin, cracking ice. *Four . . . three . . . two . . .* In this void, time slowed down. I hit against the metal fire door, frantically feeling for the handle.

A square of lighter night sky appeared in the stairwell. I gripped the window, pushing it open.

Any second now they would appear behind me. Why had they turned their flashlights off? For some reason, I found that as terrifying as being chased. I pushed my way out through the window onto the rickety fire escape, then slammed it behind me and hurried down the steps. In my panic, I felt no fear of falling. Below in the driveway I could see the headlights of Blaney's car. The radio was still playing.

"Blaney," I screamed out to her.

The car's engine revved, and the wheels slowly turned against the gravel.

"No, stop!" I looked over my shoulder at the fire escape window, still closed. I wasn't sure what was worse: the fear of their chasing me or of Blaney driving away before I reached her.

"Wait!" I screamed again as I tried to unlatch the ladder. My hands trembled. Had the metal rusted together? I tried to lift it again, but it wouldn't move. I stared down at the fourteen-foot drop. It was my only option. I climbed down as far I could, gripped the last railing and hung for a second, my feet dangling in the air. I was five six—my arms gave me another twenty-one inches before I let go. I landed on my feet but the force knocked me back onto the hardened dirt. My elbows and hands stung, but I pushed myself up and ran to Blaney's car. The driver's side window was open and I could hear the radio, some awful girl pop that she liked.

I made it. The relief hit, along with sudden exhaustion. My legs almost gave out from under me.

"Blaney," I gasped. I choked back tears of relief as I

reached for the car door handle. The passenger-side window was rolled up. Inside it was dark except for the blue glow of the phone. I yanked open the door and collapsed onto the cushion. She was leaning down into the glowing screen.

"We have to go fast!"

The woman who turned from the phone was not Blaney.

The music still blared. I froze. I was unable to move. She didn't speak. It was too dark to see anything other than her straight dark hair and angular cheekbones. Her skin appeared as white as chalk. She looked familiar, somehow. I grabbed the door handle but it was locked. I pulled up at the lock, trying to push the door open, but someone was blocking it: a man.

I was screaming but I had no idea what I was saying. I remember hearing the back door open and I thought for a moment I could escape. But the woman grabbed my wrists, pinning them to the seat. The man behind me grabbed the back of my head and neck. He was going to kill me, strangle me. My eyes grew wide.

They were weird, the thoughts that went through my head. I remembered a photograph Dad had shown me when I was little: a rabbit caught in a trap. I remember Mom was furious at him; it was one of my only clear memories of her. Why had he shown me that picture? I knew he'd had a reason . . . but it had died with him and would die with me. It had haunted me because the fear in the rabbit's eyes was so palpable. Fear and the knowledge that what was to come would be even worse.

The man had his hand on the top of my head and his arm around my neck. The woman held my wrists so tightly I felt her fingernails press into my skin. I imagined I'd pop like a balloon if her nails burst through. I lashed out kicking. I wanted to hurt her. The man tightened his grip on my neck. Blood swelled in my face, hot and dizzy. I tried to pull his arm from me but couldn't move my hands. I gasped a small amount of air when there was a tiny pinprick in my arm.

The man's grip slid away.

Keep your eyes open, I told myself. But then everything went black.

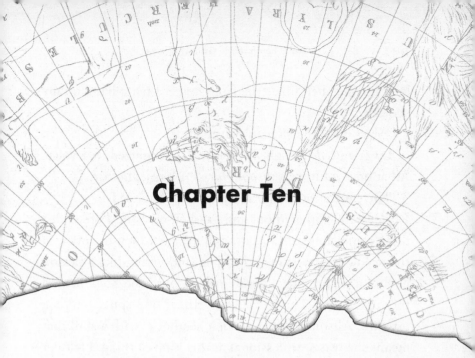

Chapter Ten

A warm feeling ran through my body, my veins. Like the sun, shining down on me. As the warmth spread, my arms went numb. The warmth turned into a tingly and unpleasant sensation. My legs felt numb, too. I couldn't move. My head felt as though it had turned to stone as my eyes stared ahead helplessly. I was aware of motion—a car on a highway—of voices, but they sounded far away, as though they were talking in another room.

Don't close your eyes, a voice warned inside my skull. It was small, like a child's, and the weight of my lids was too heavy. Something was terribly wrong; I *knew* that. But I couldn't move. I was too tired, too comfortable. I let go.

I couldn't tell how much time had passed when my eyelids fluttered open again. The feeling began to come back into my arms and legs, and with it, pain. Headlights passed in a blur from the oncoming traffic. If I had a sense of time, I would have known about how many miles we had traveled, how far they had taken me from home. I felt a hand on my shoulder.

"She's out," the woman's voice said.

I was curled up right beside her. I recognized that voice. All at once it hit me: *Alison. Harrison's receptionist.*

"Give her another shot," a man's voice replied.

Her hand slithered out and grasped my arm. I pretended to be completely asleep. Through my shirt I felt the prick of the needle hit my skin. I thrashed, mumbling like a person having a nightmare. I threw myself onto the floor behind the driver seat. The needle was still in my shirt, scraping my skin. Alison grabbed me in a headlock, with a skill that meant she was a professional at this kind of thing. I felt her press the syringe and the small amount of liquid against my skin.

"That should give us another three or four hours."

I had been asleep for three hours or more? Where were they taking me? If they wanted to kill me, why didn't they just do it now? Here. In this strange car. Were they afraid of blood, of DNA evidence? They must have moved me from Blaney's car. What had they done to her? Had they killed her back in the parking lot? I felt faint.

Some of the poison must have gotten into my bloodstream because I was losing consciousness again. Not completely, not into a dream, but almost like I was floating. But this time I was able to pull myself back. My body was too heavy once more but I forced my mind to stay awake. I wanted so badly to open my eyes to look out the car window for a road sign—anything—with which I could orient myself. So I'd know exactly how far I was from home.

• • •

I pretended to be completely blacked out from the drug. I felt the pull of direction. We were going west-southwest; the color was mostly pale blue. Why were they taking me so far if they were just going to kill me? I strained my ears, trying to listen in on their conversation. I could hear Alison, but there was another voice, too, coming through a laptop on the passenger-side front seat. At first the voice was distorted and echoing. But it, too, was vaguely familiar, an older man's voice.

"Unit D is closing in on the Alaska blueprint."

"We are near our destination," Alison replied. "Is the site secured?"

There was a pause. "Yes," the voice replied clearly.

I almost jumped up, giving myself away. *Harrison.*

It was Harrison talking through the computer. Of course; Alison was beside me. Harrison: the man my father entrusted with my life. The man whom he appointed as my godfather. The man who was supposed to protect me? It didn't seem possible, but on the other hand, none of this did. Should I try banging on the windows? What were the chances a passing car would see me? It was night, so doubtful.

Escape was the only answer. Even if it meant opening the door and jumping out onto the highway. I peeked up. A flash of the passing sky and lights from the road were all I saw. I closed my eyes quickly. Was the door locked? Too hard to tell. I would have to move to see it. Too risky.

I felt the car slow down. Heard the tick of the indicator light and felt the car turn. Going down an exit ramp? My hands grew cold. Was this it? Had I arrived at the place where

I'd be killed? I had to take my chance now. We were going more slowly. But how would I break through the window glass? I steeled myself—

Then the car came to a stop.

The smell of gasoline was distinct. They had stopped at a rest stop somewhere on the highway. With my eyes closed, faking unconsciousness, I listened.

The driver door opened and closed.

The passenger door opened and closed.

There was the chugging sound of the tank being filled. Two voices were talking outside. Then silence. There was the beep and click of the locks; the passenger door opened again. I heard a fumbling in the front seat, the brief crinkling of plastic. Then the door closed again. I waited for the beep of the lock, but didn't hear it. Was I alone in the car? I opened my eyes halfway. I was alone, but then I realized one of the men was leaning against the back passenger-side door, lighting a cigarette, using both hands to shield it from the wind. I didn't see Alison or the other man.

Cautiously I pushed myself up to look outside. I had imagined we were at one of those huge McDonald's/Shell rest stops but it was just a small gas station next to a diner. I figured the other two had gone inside to get something to eat or use the bathroom, and left the other guy to watch me. My heart leapt. The doors were unlocked. My palms felt cold and sweaty as I gripped the door handle.

That's when I saw something in the seat holder: an ice scraper. Maybe they were planning on driving north. Alison had mentioned Alaska. Were they planning on driving to Alaska? I pulled it out without thinking how I'd use it.

The man outside was fumbling to get a cigarette lit, trying to shield the lighter flame from the wind. Now I understood: He must have forgotten his smokes in the front seat. No doubt he'd lock the doors again as soon as he could. I stared out at the small white gas station, the diner with a flashing neon sign in the shape of a milk shake. There were only four other cars parked in the mostly empty lot.

Where would I go from here? Beyond the gas station was a wooded area. I couldn't see much farther. Did the woods go on for miles or were they just a patch of trees leading to someone's backyard? I assumed we must be somewhere rural, with a low population. The landscape looked flat. That made me think the trees behind the gas station might go deep and not just be in someone's backyard. My worry was that it might just be an island of trees between two highways. Where I'd be trapped.

The smoker was heavyset, dressed in a navy suit, with a head of short, grey hair. I could only see his back. I imagined he had red sweaty skin, the kind that comes from too much alcohol and meat. He wouldn't be able to outrun me. I pulled the opposite door handle, as slowly and quietly as possible, watching the man's back the whole time. He didn't hear. I crouched low and crawled out, hiding by the rear wheel.

The pavement felt hot under my palms. A breeze rustled my hair. Thank God it was summer and not freezing cold or pouring rain. There was an opening of fifty-four-plus feet between the gas station and diner. In it stood a depressing-looking Porta-Potty and a round plastic picnic table with a broken umbrella. The ground was littered with beer and soda cans. Behind that: the woods.

I sucked in a breath and took off.

My legs moved slowly from the drugs. They felt heavy and numb. The first tree, which I knew was less than sixty-nine feet from the car, seemed so far now. Using all my strength, I made it another four feet when the diner door opened and Alison came out. She carried a coffee in her hand, her cell phone in the other. She froze for a split second, staring at me before she pulled something from her pocket.

I hurled the ice scraper at her. I watched in amazement as it spun in the air like a boomerang, hitting the side of her head. The coffee spilled over her hand and she shouted in pain. The heavyset man guarding the car looked up from his cell phone. I didn't look back, but I could hear him running after me.

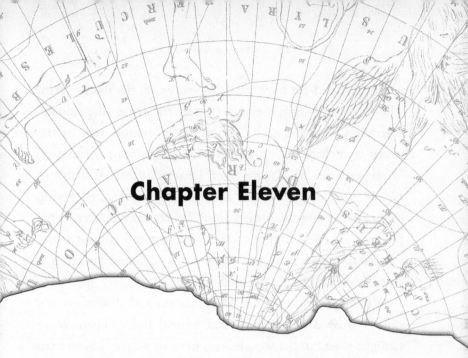

Chapter Eleven

The woods are dark on a cloudless night. It must have been the adrenaline that made me sprint in near blindness when just a few seconds ago my legs felt like lead.

I stopped when I heard a strange thud, and then another, and another. Bark exploded off the trees around me. Wisps of smoke rose from tiny black holes in the trunks. I stared for a moment, frozen, stupefied.

They're shooting at me.

Another pop, and I dove to the rough ground, crawling forward on my hands and knees. There was no sound of gunshots. That's what Alison had pulled from her pocket, a gun with a silencer. I held my breath. Flashlights swept through the branches. I could hear footsteps over the crunching leaves, the heavy sound of breathing, the voices of the two men. How far away were they? I couldn't know if I couldn't see them. I pushed myself up, running again. More bullets. I ducked, stumbling over a tree root—and fell.

They would get me now. I lay frozen on the damp earth. The beams of light swept through the trees like ghosts. Their footsteps drew closer and closer, punctuated by the sharp crunch of leaves. I pressed my face against the dirt, holding my breath. *Please God,* I prayed, *don't let them see me.* In a panic, I grabbed a handful of acorns, throwing them in the opposite direction. When they clattered off the trees, the flashlights suddenly swung toward the noise. I dared to lift my head, watching as they hurried toward it.

"She's over here!" Alison shouted.

Without thinking, I bolted. Branches and thorns cut my skin. I tripped in burrows and animal holes. There is no straight ahead in the woods; you have to weave. They heard my footsteps because in an instant, they were right behind me again, hunting me.

That's when I fell.

The drop seemed to take forever: feet first, down and down. My back hit against the roots and rocks. I grabbed at the dirt, reaching for anything to still myself, to hold on to. I couldn't see above or below me. I landed with a sharp jolt and fell forward onto my hands and knees, knocked out of breath and stunned with fear.

I couldn't see anything. I was too afraid to move. Was there flat land around me? Or was there another slope or cliff a few feet away?

I looked up; the sky was starless. I looked down; the ground was black. The only sound I could hear was my pulse in my head and ears. My first instinct was to scream for help but the only people who would hear were the ones I was running from. I stayed still, listening to my frantic heartbeat. I looked around; they were gone. No voices, no flashlights, no bullets, no footsteps. Had they given up and assumed I was dead?

I'm lost. I'm completely alone. I am hurt.

Knowing this was more frightening than anything else that had happened to me. More frightening than the car, the bullets, the chase.

The air felt cool, even cold against my skin. Different animals made sudden, quick noises around me. I curled my legs into my chest and wrapped my arms around them. A burning sensation seared my left ankle from the fall. I squinted through the ravine, searching for any sign of lights. There were none. Have you ever seen a map of the world at night? Africa is red with fires; North Korea is black; America is dotted with crystal white blobs. How far was I from one of those?

My mouth was parched and filled with the metallic taste of blood. I curled up against the base of a tree. My left ankle burned like a flame. I was too tired even to cry.

The sky was grey-blue when I woke up. At first I had no recollection of where I was. I stared at the earth, the leaves, the endless trees in disbelief. Just yesterday I had woken up in my own bed and now I was in a dry creek bed in the woods, lost, far from home. Somewhere I could hear the tinkling sound of water.

I pushed myself up. My head ached, I was thirsty and dizzy. At least the pain in my ankle had subsided. The palms of my hands were bloody and scuffed from where I'd fallen, and I knew I had to rinse the dirt away from the broken skin as soon as possible. My jeans were ripped at the knee and covered in dirt and leaves. I looked like a child who'd taken a terrible spill on the playground. But I wasn't a child and this wasn't a fall from a bike or roller skates.

Behind me the earth rose at a steep angle, twenty-three feet up to a ridge, scarred by my path. That fall might have saved my life. The creek wasn't entirely dry; seventeen feet to my right was a small stream of water running slowly over the rocks. In the dawn it looked crystal clear.

I had never been so happy to see water before. I limped over to it. I knew my ankle wasn't broken, though. I knelt down and let the icy water rinse the dirt and blood from my scraped hands. I cupped them and gulped feverishly, spilling all over myself. Water had never tasted so good, so clean and cold. I washed my face and wiped the dirt from my jeans and the navy sweatshirt I had on. Then I took off my sneakers and socks and soaked my feet and ankle, hoping it would stop the swelling and pain.

Birds chirped overhead. I realized I was panting. But I felt human again. Now I had to find my way out of the woods. I stood up. The sun was just climbing over the treetops. I figured it was about eight A.M. I turned myself in a circle. The ravine wall blocked my path back to the gas station, but I didn't want to go there. They might still be waiting for me. I marked the tree I'd slept against with a rock, carving a double line in the bark and headed northeast, toward home, measuring in my head as I went.

I counted two hundred yards, marked another tree, and limped another two hundred yards, marked another tree and walked another two hundred steps. My stomach sunk in with hunger, my ankle ached, I couldn't stop thinking about grapefruit juice and a grilled cheese sandwich. I imagined I'd find an ace bandage on the ground.

A thousand yards became two thousand. I fought back a tide of panic. The woods were endless. Was Blaney looking for me? The police? Beth? I knew she was and she must be worried sick. Harrison, my father's best friend, my legal guardian, had been talking to the people who'd taken me— unless I'd mistaken his voice on the computer. I wasn't sure what was real or not anymore.

"Hello!" I yelled to the sky. "Hello! Help me!"

The sun was overhead now; it was midday.

For a few hours, I'd managed to hope, but now I was losing it. I could be in a national park. I pictured the map of the eastern states, those green areas, how they were so small compared to the towns and villages.

I turned due east, toward the coast. The pain in my ankle was like a person screaming in my ear. Maybe Alison and the men had left me because they'd known I'd get lost and die. I was so afraid of the unknown. I'd never been lost. I was more afraid now than when I'd been taken in the car.

"Hello!" I tried to scream again. "Help me! Help!"

Plowing eastward, I caught a glimpse of something lying beneath the leaves. It was orange, plastic. I kicked the leaves away with my foot: an orange Nerf machine gun, a child's toy. Quickly I searched for a path, a disruption in the leaves or footsteps in the mud. Nothing was clear. I walked ten steps due south, then another ten, still nothing. If a child was playing in the woods there must be a house nearby. Maybe?

This was hope. I heard the sound of wind again, waiting

to feel it or see it in the branches and leaves but the leaves were still. I turned around and glimpsed a foam orange bullet. The ground to the north-northwest looked trampled. Fourteen yards in that direction, I saw a second Nerf bullet lying in the leaves.

The sound of the wind came, but there was no breeze.

It wasn't the wind I was hearing. It was a car. It was so faint, though. I froze, waiting. *There . . .*

My ankle burned but I ran. Marking where I'd been before so I didn't waste any time retracing my steps. With the falling leaves and the muddy ground, everything looked the same. That's when I saw the third bullet and the clearing light.

I stopped, catching my breath. I shifted all my weight to one foot. In front of me the trees thinned, a dirt trail no more than a foot wide cut through the woods. NO TRESPASSING signs were nailed to the trees, a fire pit was dug into the ground, filled with charred wood. Cigarette butts and beer bottles littered the ground. I'd never been so happy to see signs of human life.

The path came to a clearing and a red clapboard house.

I'm safe, I thought. *I'm safe now.*

In the dusk, the red house looked like home. I imagined a family in the kitchen, eating dinner. I walked past the plastic wading pool, its turquoise faded from the sun and the water filled with fallen leaves. A child's bike lay on the ground, the wheels missing. As I drew closer, the story I would tell the nice family inside played on fast-forward: *I am lost. I am in danger. Call the police and call my stepmother.* They would take me in, feed me, act concerned to mask their initial fear of a strange and filthy teenager showing up from their back-yard unannounced. And then they would make the calls.

A silver-colored car was parked in a dirt drive. It had a Virginia license plate. I was in Virginia? As I drew closer, I saw that the red paint on the house was chipped in many places, marred with ugly stains. The blinds were drawn in the upstairs windows; the two downstairs windows were boarded up with plywood. Through the screen in the back door I could see a bare light bulb burning in the kitchen.

I walked up the back steps. I felt an overwhelming mixture of fear, hunger, and thirst. I couldn't tell if I was hot or cold. I held my hand in my sweatshirt pocket. That joy when I first saw the house from the woods, like finding a gold coin, was gone. I tapped on the screen door, overcome with my need to find someone, *anyone*, to help me.

There were sounds—indistinct voices and footsteps upstairs—but no one answered. On the round table inside the kitchen, an ashtray, I could see a pack of cigarettes and beer cans. A pot cooked on the stove. My nose wrinkled at the strange metallic smell that came through the screen.

Now I had a bad feeling. Showing up here might be more dangerous than being alone. There were clearly people in the house, and they didn't want to be found.

I looked toward the road. No other house in sight.

Just go. Just keep going.

I counted in my head to the number seventeen. This was something I hadn't done in years. It started as a nervous tic after Mom died, because I knew it was exactly seventeen feet total from the foot of my bed to the foot of my father's bed.

When I'd finished counting, the voices upstairs grew to a

shout. I walked away without thinking, quickly toward the road. I didn't know which way to go: left or right? It was lighter to the left, so I went southwest toward the setting sun, following the downward slope of the hill. There were no lights, no other houses. I moved quickly, even running in short spurts until the pain in my ankle made it impossible.

I guessed I had forty-five minutes before dark. I felt my right side pocket. I had some cash and my bank card. Thank God Beth had always warned me to keep some money "on your person." Thank God I'd followed her advice. Thank God for Beth . . .

My wallet was in my canvas shoulder bag—back at my cubicle along with my phone. Pathetic, but I was lost without my phone. Did I even have anyone's number memorized? My brain came up empty. I hadn't eaten anything since I'd left MapOut. Like a broken clock, my mind kept ticking back to lunchtime at work Friday, asking WHY I hadn't eaten both halves of the sandwich I'd packed, remembering how I'd thrown the brown crusts and leftover peanut butter into the woods for the birds.

The dirt road cut between two overgrown, untended fields. I hurried along it, limping now with every step. The light was turning a greyish purple. A flock of birds flew in a V overhead, heading northeast, carried by the wind. Every step I took tore at my ankle. As I staggered in the near dark, I made a list in my head: aspirin, ace bandage, water, food, call Beth . . .

No, I had to call the police first. I knew Beth would be going crazy, worried sick. But what about Blaney? What had they done to her? Did they kill her? Kidnap her?

I stiffened.

An unmistakable distant sound cut across the dirt road: the long muted blast of a train horn. I ran toward it until a single pair of headlights rushed into view and vanished in the distance. Then I sprinted, trying to ignore the pain in my ankle. *When I get there, then I'll be safe.* My legs burned when I finally reached the paved road of a town.

I'm not sure how long I stood at the town's edge. Beyond the crossing were the lights of storefronts. A spire stood dark against the night. At first I thought it was a church steeple, but as I walked closer it looked like a castle or fortress. I blinked several times, fighting fatigue. The light turned green and I concentrated on walking a straight line, toward a lighted pizza sign.

As soon as I pulled open the glass door, my mouth watered. I counted the money in my pocket: twenty-six dollars plus some change and my bank card. Hunger overrode anything else: my fear for Blaney, my concern for Beth, thoughts of Connor.

And then I glimpsed myself in the mirror on the back wall.

My hair was ratty, clumped, my hands and face smeared with dirt. The rip that ran down the side of my jeans—torn from the fall in the ravine—was stained with brownish spots of blood. My eyes widened at the unrecognizable reflection. This wasn't just a homeless girl; this was a filthy, crazy vagrant. Someone who might be dangerous. Me.

The fat bald man behind the counter asked for the money before he handed me two slices on a paper plate and a bottle of water. I couldn't blame him. He eyed me suspiciously as I sunk into a corner booth. What happened next was a blur of starvation; I inhaled the pizza and the water. Only when I'd finished did I notice the other people around me: four kids my age on a double date, talking about a baseball game. The girls were wearing the boys' jackets, maroon and blue. ALTON HIGH FOOTBALL.

I was in Alton, Virginia.

For the first time since I'd escaped the car, I could think clearly again. I yawned. My stomach felt unsettled, but a warm, delicious drowsiness suddenly rose up from deep inside. I thought about curling up in the booth cushion.

Fighting the impulse, I rubbed my eyes, hard. I pictured Alison as she injected me, the expressionless look on her face as she pulled out the gun. Why would they have killed me in the woods, but not in the car? They hadn't followed me down the ravine, so I doubted I could be traced. They had my phone; I hadn't used my bank card. Not yet, at least. But I couldn't assume they gave me up for dead or lost forever.

In the tiny bathroom of the pizza place, I cleaned up as much as I could. I scrubbed my face with the foam from the grimy dispenser. I tried to wipe the dirt and bloodstains from my clothes with a damp paper towel, but only ended up smearing the mud around my dirty clothes.

When I combed my hair with my fingers, I noticed my hands were shaking. They were still shaking when I left, the fat bald guy staring at me.

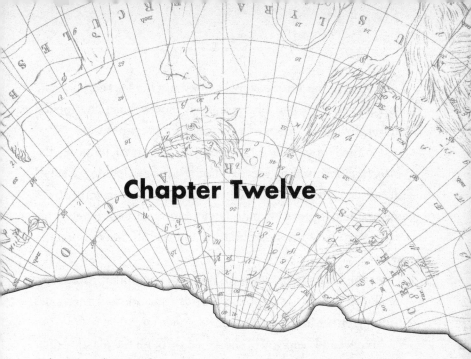

Chapter Twelve

I'd mapped enough towns to know that most had a police station, a post office, and a church, so I took my chances and walked toward the castle-like steeple. The night wasn't cold, but I kept shivering. After a few blocks I hit Main Street: rows of impressive eighteenth-century buildings wrought with decorative stone, probably once banks or grand department stores, now mostly dark or boarded up. I knew this small-town story well. At MapOut we weren't just putting new places, things, shops, and restaurants on the Map—we were also taking them off, erasing them. In some towns, Main Street vanished completely when a Walmart appeared down the highway.

Above the massive double doors on the castle-like fortress, in line with the steeple high above, was a pair of stone engravings: ALTON TOWN HALL and POLICE STATION. Rows of small square windows made the whole place seem especially forbidding, and for a second I wondered if this were also a jail.

Two girls sat on the steps, smoking. One looked up at me as I passed. She had blue eyes and blonde hair; she looked about my age or younger, and was very pregnant.

I pulled open one of the doors, the smell of pine disinfectant reminding me of middle school. Inside, a small fluorescent-lit antechamber was packed with a half-dozen miserable people. One man held a bloodstained towel to his arm. Posters of missing children and sex offenders lined the walls.

At the far end was a booth, protected by bulletproof glass. A plump woman in a police uniform sat on the other side, looking either angry or bored.

"How can I help you?" she asked through the plastic grate.

"I need to talk to a police officer." My voice shook. "I need to report a crime."

"You need to report a crime," the woman repeated. Her tone was flat. She reached forward, taking a yellow piece of paper from a tray of pastel-colored forms. "Fill this out," she said, pushing it through an opening slot.

"I have to fill out a form?"

"Yes, you do."

"Can't I just tell you what happened to me? Or talk—"

"Fill out the form," she snapped.

I glared at her. I had been drugged, kidnapped, people had tried to shoot me. Now was the time for the law to come running to my rescue. I scribbled as quickly as I could.

Name: Tanya Blue Barrett
Date of reported crime: June 25
Description of reported crime: kidnapping

The details were barely legible, but I didn't care. As soon as I was done, I slid it back under the bulletproof glass. The woman glanced at it and slid off her stool. After what seemed like an eternity, a side door opened and a male police officer stepped into the hall. He was greying, rugged, paunchy, maybe Beth's age.

"Tanya Barrett?" he grunted.

"That's me," I said, my voice a cracked whisper. My heart raced as I followed him through a door marked DETECTIVE WARREN MORRIS.

I followed him into the tiny office. There was no place for me to sit. He slumped down in his desk chair and glanced over the yellow report I'd filled out. My eyes wandered to a navy mug, printed with PROUD PARENT OF AN ALTON HIGH HONOR STUDENT. A gold-framed photograph of two children, a boy and a girl, sat beside it on his desk. In the picture the boy looked about twelve and the girl fourteen. She had a pretty face, brown hair pulled back, and a big smile with braces.

"You reported that you were kidnapped, drugged, taken in a car, shot at . . ."

He kept his eyes on the paper. His hands and face looked dried and weather-beaten.

"It's true." I spoke quickly. The words poured out in a frenzied rush as I retold the story I'd summarized on the paper: how I'd been at MapOut working late when the electricity was cut off, and how I'd gotten into the car thinking it was my friend Blaney . . .

"That's enough." He held his hand up to stop me.

"What?" I felt myself fighting back tears.

He pressed a button on the printer beside the computer

screen, then leaned back in the chair and finally looked me in the eye. "Tanya," he said. "Do you know there's a warrant out for your arrest?" He picked up a white sheet of paper from the printer tray and held it out to show me.

MISSING CHILD

NAME: TANYA BARRETT

Last seen leaving 46 Maple Street, Amherst, MA, at 9 P.M., getting into blue Volkswagen.

Age: 16

Hair: Brown.

Eyes: Brown.

Height: 5'6"

Weight: 115 lb.

Wanted for breaking and entering. Computer hacking and robbery. If anyone has information regarding this child, contact: Commissioner John Kelly of the Amherst Police Department, 413-880-8866.

I stared at my face in black-and-white pixels, my class picture from last year. Then it hit me. Harrison had reported me to the police for hacking into my dad's files. I flashed back to that terrible moment in his office when he confronted me about the incident, warning me that what I had done was a criminal act. I couldn't breathe.

The detective looked at me with a sorry expression. He folded his hands on his desk, leaning forward. "I have a daughter your age. I hate to see someone so young in this position. There are options for girls like you. Rehab is one."

"Rehab?"

"You came from Massachusetts to these parts for a reason, I'd wager. You probably know as well as I do how much meth moves in and out of Alton."

My mind flashed to that crumbling red house at the edge of the woods, that sickly metallic smell wafting from its kitchen. He thought I was a drug addict, a runaway, a delinquent. "You don't understand; this . . ." I tried to explain but choked on the words.

He handed me a box of tissues. "We'll have to keep you here in the holding cell until your legal guardian claims you. Your guardian or the court decides what to do."

For a moment I was too panicked to speak. I sniffed and wiped my eyes, fighting to remain calm. "Can I call my mom?" I managed. I wasn't about to tell him both my parents were dead. That would help confirm the suspicion he'd already formed thanks to Harrison, that I was some street kid who broke into buildings to steal computers.

I clenched the tissue in one fist as Detective Morris shoved his phone toward me. My hand felt clammy as I clutched the receiver, jabbing at the buttons with my forefinger. Thank God I could remember the number. It was my mom's number.

My dad's number. The only number that had never changed. I pressed the black, heavy receiver to my ear. It smelled faintly of cologne. It rang once.

"Hello?" Beth answered, her voice frantic.

"Beth?"

"Tanya," she gasped. "Oh, thank heaven. Where have you been? Where are you? Blaney told me she was waiting for you but you never showed up . . ."

"Blaney told you? You saw Blaney? She's okay?" I let out a sigh of relief that echoed Beth's.

"She's fine, but where are you?"

"I'm at a police station," I told her as calmly as I could. "There's a warrant out for my arrest. They're going to put me in jail."

Beth paused. "What police station? Where?"

"Alton—"

"Tanya," a voice interrupted.

I froze. *Harrison. He's with Beth.* And I had said my location by name.

"Tanya," Harrison repeated. "Where are you?"

I couldn't speak. He spoke in the same quiet and commanding tone he'd used when speaking to my kidnappers through the computer in the car. My throat felt thick. Who were these people who supposedly loved me, who were meant to be looking after me, these people whom my father had trusted with my life? I slammed the phone down on the hook. I had nowhere to go. No one to go to. Home was not an option. Home didn't even exist anymore, apparently.

"Are you okay?" Detective Morris asked.

"I'm sorry, I . . . um—I need the bathroom," I stammered.

A flash of what looked like sympathy crossed his face. He chewed his lip. "To the left, at the end of the hall," he said. "Don't take too long."

As if in a dream, I shambled out and headed toward the battered lavatory door. On my right, I passed a door marked JANITORIAL.

Something in my brain clicked into gear.

The janitor's door was parallel to the entrance. It was exactly twelve feet from the front wall, where I'd noticed those strange prison-like square windows. I hesitated, remembering there had been nothing behind them; the glass was dark like water at night, which probably meant the room was empty. No one was watching me. I glanced back toward Detective Morris's office, then tried the door handle as quietly as I could.

It opened.

In a flash, I shut the door behind me, engulfed in pitch-blackness.

The air smelled of mildew and bleach, and worse. I felt the doorjamb for an inside lock but there was none. I knew I didn't have time; I knew I'd be found. I blinked and squinted, willing my eyes to adjust. But even after several minutes, I couldn't make out anything more than vague silhouettes, shapes at an indeterminate distance.

Steeling myself, I backed against the door and walked forward slowly into nothingness, hands in front of me, blind. My fingertips brushed against something soft and plastic. Paper towels. Rolls of them. My hands dropped and landed on a shelf. Gripping the edge tightly, I moved to the right until I reached the shelf's end. I was able to move past it, toward the outer wall. I was seven feet from those windows now. Hands back in front of me, I stepped forward.

"Tanya?" Detective Morris barked from the hall.

I froze as his footsteps pounded past the closet. He rapped loudly on the bathroom door. My heart thumped. I reached to the left and found the back of the paper towel shelves, then inched farther to the left. A foul stench tickled my nostrils. I made it six feet before I nearly tripped over a huge plastic mass of something.

"Tanya, open up!" he barked.

"What's going on, Warren?" a female voice asked. It sounded gravelly, like the woman behind the bulletproof glass. But it could have belonged to anyone.

"I let her go to the bathroom," the detective grumbled.

"Alone? Why didn't you call me?"

"Just open the damn door, Beatrice."

I held my breath and heard the creak of hinges. "It's open," the woman spat.

"Jesus Christ," he whispered.

"You left the side door open when you went for your coffee break, too. Remember that, genius? She's probably hitchhiked halfway to Richmond by now."

"Shut up; she can't be far. Check the supply closet."

Without thinking, I crouched down low.

The door flew open, and the sudden flood of light made me wince. In an instant, I assessed my surroundings: I was huddled between two tall banks of cleaning supply shelves, right next to an industrial-sized bag of rotting garbage. No wonder this room smelled so bad. Hiding behind the bag was my only option. I straddled it and lay down on my knees, squeezing my ankles under my butt, prostrating myself so my forehead touched the dank stone floor. I knew from the size of the bag and the size of my body I'd be invisible to anyone who peeked between the shelves. Of course, if anyone bothered to look closely at all, I'd be caught . . .

The putrid stench was overpowering. My pulse raced so hard that I barely heard the scuffling of the officer's feet, up to the outer wall and back toward the hall again.

"She ain't here," she called. "Jesus, it stinks. When was the last time you cleaned this place, Warren? What the hell is going on with you, anyway?"

The door slammed shut, enveloping me once more in blackness.

My breath came in gasps. I concentrated on relaxing the flow of awful-smelling air in and out of my lungs. I counted to seventeen over and over again—five, six, seven times. When I could no longer hear their voices or footsteps, I crawled back over the bag. I decided to stay low just in case the door opened again. Back on my hands and knees, I felt my way out of the passage between the shelves. The dank floor was sticky in places. I ignored the grime, ignored the smell, ignored my fear.

Turning left I scrambled the last four feet eight inches to the wall. At the bottom I felt a draft from above. With it, relief washed over me. But when I stood and felt for the glass, my fingers bumped up against a square metal plate.

The windows were sealed with some kind of latch. I ran my hand along the edge and felt a bolt. It was stuck. I pushed again. It wouldn't budge.

The sound of a police siren echoed outside. Why were the windows bolted shut? What would I do now? I was trapped. Hidden, but trapped. But of course I was. This was a police station. Detective Morris may have been careless in leaving a door open, but an entire police department wouldn't be stupid. If they detained people in this building, they would seal off any room that could provide an escape.

Calm down, I said to myself. *Calm down and think. Think. The side door may still be open. Maybe I can get out that way.*

My hands went cold and I felt a pain in my chest. I couldn't keep still, but there was no room to pace. That's what panic does: it forces you further and further into danger, further into your own mind. I mustered all my strength, pushing against the bolt until my palms were blistered and sore. When I brought them to my face, they smelled of metal and rust. I screamed silently into my hands.

The enormity of the situation hit. Even if I miraculously escaped, I wasn't safe. Harrison was hunting me for a reason I couldn't even begin to guess. Harrison, the man who was my "second dad." What had I done wrong? I tried the latch again. *This time, by some magical turn of events, it will open.* I remembered Beth once telling me that the definition of insanity is when you try the same thing over and over, expecting different results.

I slid down the wall. Squeezing my eyes shut, I rocked

back and forth, wracked with silent sobs. My ankle ached again. It was swollen, hot to the touch, but massaging it made it feel slightly better. The temptation to give up and scream for help bubbled from some desperate place. There was no other way this could end. I'd be caught.

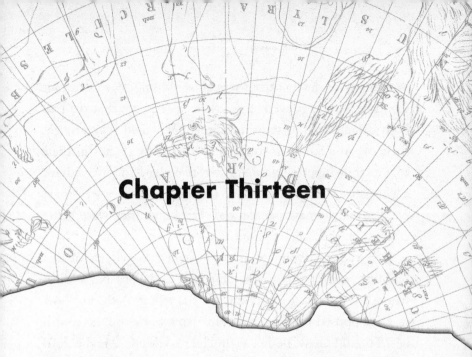

Chapter Thirteen

When I jerked awake, my first thought was that I needed to use the bathroom. Badly. For a moment I forgot where I was. But the whiff of garbage and the cold grimy floor beneath my cheek brought me back in a queasy rush. I bolted upright, my eyes drawn to thin strips of light above me: sunshine peeking through the bolted metal shutters. I listened to the sounds on the street outside, birds chirping, the rumble of trucks, car doors opening and closing. In the distance, I could just barely make out the steady, unmistakable clatter of a train.

It must have been Sunday, but I had no idea what time. My first thought was, *I have to get back to MapOut by Monday morning for work*. I imagined myself on my bike, riding into the MapOut parking lot. All those bright college kids would be locking up their bikes and getting ready for the day. Then, it hit me: that was not my reality anymore I wondered if any of those college kids had any idea who their boss really was.

Would any of them notice I was gone? Would they ask about Connor? Would it even strike them as strange that we had both disappeared at the same time? Or would they just get their organic Sumatra coffee and plug their iTunes in their ears as they inputted data and wrote code? Did anyone have a clue about what was going on there? These were smart people, really smart people, did they know they were being clocked on their smart phones?

I shoved the thoughts aside. I needed to get out of this building, out of this town. Harrison and Beth both knew where I was now. I kicked myself for telling Beth, but how was I supposed to know that Harrison would be there with her? For all I knew, Beth was on Harrison's side. Maybe she'd told Alison to go ahead and shoot. I thought of the movie *Rosemary's Baby*, one of Dad's favorites. That's the way my life felt right now: every person close to me was in on the same conspiracy. There was almost no one I could trust. And the few I could, like Rebs or Blaney, I'd jeopardize.

The rest, like my mom and dad, were dead.

I pushed myself to my feet and gingerly tested my ankle. It wasn't nearly as sore as it had been. But my joints were stiff and my back ached from sleeping on the floor. Using the lavatory was too risky, so I held my breath, ducking behind the sack of garbage where I'd hid last night. It was amazing how quickly my eyes adjusted to the tiny bit of sunlight leaking through those cracks. A moment later, I stepped out from between the two supply shelves—and my gaze zeroed in on a box beside the door.

Written in black marker across it were the words LOST & FOUND. I rifled through it, tossing aside a brown flip-flop, a brown winter coat, a pair of sunglasses, a purple hair scrunchie. Did girls still wear scrunchies in Alton? A Frisbee, a Redskins cap, a purple-blue Alton High sweatshirt. I held it up; it was a little big but it would work. I pulled off my filthy grey hoodie and buried it in the bottom of the pile, then pulled the sweatshirt over my head. It smelled surprisingly clean, of detergent. I pressed the fabric to my nose, taking a deep breath. It reminded me of home, the home I no longer had.

With a pang, I pushed my hair back, tying it up with the purple scrunchie. Then I grabbed the baseball cap and pulled the ponytail through the back. Not my favorite look, but whatever; I didn't want to look like me. What I really needed was a new pair of pants. Mine were ripped, not in the right places, and mud-stained.

Time to go.

I was banking on two things. The first: Detective Morris probably worked the night shift, so his office would be deserted. I closed my eyes, picturing the route back to the main entrance. It was right there in my memory. I counted the steps through the halls and back into the foyer with the bulletproof glass. Not far: left, right, then left again—a total of 34 feet. The second: it was early, so maybe the police station would be quiet. Maybe that gravel-voiced woman would be home, too.

Overhearing even a single voice out there would mean a dead end. I couldn't count on finding that side exit; besides, it was probably alarmed or locked now. When I studied real maps, I was always looking for a way from A to B, a way in, a way out, a way to connect one road to another, a way over, a way under. Mapmakers don't like dead ends.

Dead ends, my dad used to say, were a mapmaker's worst enemy.

I pressed my ear to the door. Silence. Still I hesitated; this was all about timing.

When I was certain that all I could hear were birds chirping and distant traffic behind me, I turned the knob, pulling open the door. My eyes stung from the light, a visceral pain, as if I were staring at the sun. There was no time to hesitate. Head down, I threaded my way through the station, past Detective Morris's darkened office.

The halls were silent. But when I opened the foyer door, I nearly froze.

A young mother and her toddler were whispering on one of the benches. A round, black-and-white clock ticked above the front doors; I hadn't noticed it before. It was 8:27, later than I thought. To my right, two uniformed police officers stood by the bulletproof glass. A different woman, a thin brunette, sat behind it now. The officers drank coffee from white Styrofoam cups and laughed about something with her.

Walk normally, not too slow, not too fast. Act like you know what you're doing.

Panic was a rushing wave that threatened to cut my wobbly legs out from under me. I forced myself toward the door. As I passed the posters of missing children, I glimpsed a new addition tacked on among them: TANYA BARRETT. It had no effect. The pixelated, fresh-faced, happy-looking girl with my name was a stranger to me.

Pushing open the doors into the bright summer sunshine, I kept my pace even as I walked down the steps. Nobody called after me. I'd made it out. I even felt a surge of something like hope, because the picture had clarified something. Harrison reported me to the police to cover himself. The police would never believe my crazy story against his.

And it struck me: my issues with Beth notwithstanding, I knew she'd never hurt me. She couldn't have been on Harrison's side. Nobody could fake the kind of pain she'd suffered over my dad's death; nobody would tend to an orphaned daughter if they didn't feel even a trace of compassion. No, Harrison had pretended to Beth that he loved and cared about me, his surrogate daughter—that he was just as desperate for me to return as she was.

Maybe the girl in the picture would have believed him and run back to the safety of her house. But that girl didn't exist anymore. I had to leave her and Alton far behind.

Twenty minutes later, I was inside the small Alton train station and bus terminal. It had been easy, almost intuitive to find. I went straight for the Dunkin' Donuts stand, pulled by the smell of coffee. The green lines of the Peter Pan schedule blurred and swam in front of my eyes as I waited in line. In my pocket were twenty-two dollars and my bank card. The bus I wanted, the one heading to Chicago, was leaving at 9:15.

It was 8:57 A.M. I knew I should save every last cent, but I was exhausted and hungry. I ordered the breakfast special, a medium coffee and an egg and cheese on a roll, for $3.19. As I paid the cashier, I spied two police officers—the same two I'd seen back at the station—walking through the double glass doors. From the corner of my eye, I observed as they moved slowly, surveying the scene.

I slid into a corner table, sitting with my back to them. My hands shook as I brought the coffee to my lips and hot liquid spilled down my fingers and wrists.

I could do this. I could make it. I had a plan now.

On the short walk here, I'd fought to organize my thoughts into what I did know and what I didn't. What I knew: Harrison was trying to kill me. What I didn't know: how to find Connor. What I did know . . . not much else. Except for one thing—that the only other person who might have a clue as to the truth was Cleo, and when I'd called her, she'd sounded scared.

It was all I had, so it would have to be enough.

Somehow, she and Alaska (whatever that was) and the attempt on my life were all related. I stared down at the linoleum table, imagining the white-and-lime-green marbled pattern turning to roads and rail lines, stretching from Virginia to New Mexico, via Chicago. The entire trip would take close to three days. Thirteen hours by bus to Union Station—a big-city hub, a place I could disappear, at least for a little while—and another forty-eight by train to Elk, New Mexico.

When I finished my coffee, I turned my head as cautiously as I could. The police officers were gone. I headed straight to the ticket counter to ask the price of the ticket to Chicago. Eighty dollars. Then I asked the price of a ticket to Boston. Forty-five. My plan was to buy two tickets: first, one for Boston under my name, one that would leave an obvious trail. I was sure that if Harrison really wanted to find me, he would be able to track me in real time. The easiest way for him to do this would be through my electronic footprint, when I checked my emails or withdrew money

from an ATM. It was why I hadn't even considered finding
an Internet café to check email or contact anyone; it was
why, even though there was an ATM twenty feet away from
me, I hadn't used it.

The huge clock above the ticket counter read 9:03. The
bus to Chicago would leave in twelve minutes. The bus to
Boston left in twenty-seven.

Once again I wondered what Harrison could possibly be
up to. Maybe he was a drug dealer. Detective Morris had
mentioned that this was a big meth area; maybe it *wasn't* a
coincidence that Alison and my other kidnappers had driven
me to Virginia. Maybe they were planning to boil me alive
in a giant meth pot. Maybe that's where Harrison got the
money to do those renovations; maybe Rytech had nothing
to do with it. But even as the thought occurred to me, it
seemed like a stretch. Harrison wasn't one of the guys from
Breaking Bad, and those working for him struck me as too
sophisticated for that kind of crime. Besides, Dad would have
suspected something.

The clock ticked with infinite slowness.

Finally, at 9:11, I marched over to the ATM and shoved my
card in the slot. For all I knew, my bank account could have
been hacked into and shut down. It had been stupid to buy
breakfast. But no, the $2,400 in my savings account popped
up on the screen. I was good at saving money. The bulk of
what I'd earned at camp the previous summers had been squir-
reled away here. I prayed I could withdraw all $2,400 now.

I punched in $2,000.

A message popped up: DAILY MAXIMUM WITHDRAWAL
IS $300.

Okay. Calm down. I knew that.

I looked at the clock: 9:12. The Chicago bus was leaving in three minutes.

I punched in $300.

A $3.00 CHARGE WILL BE PROCESSED FOR THIS WITHDRAWAL.

I hit CONTINUE. The minute hand ticked to 11:13. The machine made clicking sounds. "Come on, come on," I muttered, slamming my fist against the plastic. Finally, the money slid into the dispenser. I gripped the bills tightly as I ran to the counter and asked the ticket lady for a one-way to Boston.

She asked me my name.

"Tanya Barrett," I said, loud and clear as she typed. A black video camera hung from the corner of the wall. "T-A-N-Y-A B-A-R-R-E-T-T," I spelled out.

Taking the ticket, I ran out to Gate 5. The bus to Chicago was still boarding.

A young mother, not much older than me, wearing lots of makeup and a short skirt, was holding the hand of a little girl. Both were bony, pale. They didn't have suitcases, just a plastic garbage bag for their belongings. I sidled up to them. The girl stared up at me with wide brown eyes. She carried a naked baby doll in her arms.

"How much was your ticket?" I asked the mother breathlessly.

"Eighty bucks. My daughter's free. The ticket office is inside." Her voice was gruff. She gestured with her chin.

"I'll give you two hundred for it right now."

The woman looked baffled. "What? Why? Are you trying to scam me?" She sneered and gave me a once-over, her eyes narrowing at my torn jeans.

"It's too complicated to explain. Please. But I need to be on that bus. If you can wait until the next one . . ." I showed her the money.

"You sure? Crazy girl," she mumbled under her breath. But she smiled. Several teeth were missing; the ones that remained were yellow and rotted. She gave me her ticket and I handed her the money. I read her name: COURTNEY FRANK.

An old man with a cane, pulling a suitcase on wheels, walked ahead of me up the steps of the bus. I followed behind him and found a spot across from him in the back.

Sinking into the tattered cushioned seat was pure relief. I closed my eyes for a moment. My ankle had started to burn again. I had slept maybe seven hours in the last two days. I felt dirty and sticky, and my underarms smelled. I hoped no one besides the real Courtney Frank would notice. Fortunately the old man was already snoring. I prayed he'd remain that way until Chicago.

It would be a long bus ride and I knew I'd be nervous the entire time. I'd be nervous the rest of my life. I had no idea if I was making the right choice or not, but I didn't have any other choice to make. After another minute or two, I opened my eyes. Out the window, I spotted Courtney Frank yanking her sobbing daughter into a battered sedan. For a moment, I wondered if they were headed off somewhere to spend their newfound money on drugs.

As they left, another car pulled into the bus station parking lot: a grey Lexus.

My breath caught in my throat. I'd never seen the car before, but the woman driving it looked like Alison. From the height of my seat and the angle, I could see directly into the car's windshield. *It's her.* She had the same straight dark hair; it fell forward, obscuring her face as she studied an iPad. Next to her sat a police officer I recognized instantly: Detective Morris.

I turned away from the window, heart thumping, and rubbed my clammy hands over what was left of my pants. The driver stood outside the open bus doors, counting the tickets. I looked around at the other passengers, trying to determine if anyone else looked concerned or suspicious. More than five minutes had passed since I'd bought my ticket. Either the buses here didn't run on time, or this one was being held.

The driver's-side door of the grey Lexus opened. The woman stepped out, cell phone pressed to her ear; the breeze blew her hair away from her face. That pale skin, those sharply arched eyebrows, that narrow slope of the nose—it was Alison, unmistakably, long since showered and rested after her attempt to hunt me down. She stood less than 50 feet from the bus.

I jumped up and hurried to the bathroom. The handle wouldn't turn.

Occupied.

The old man was awake and looking at me now.

"Excuse me?" I said, trying to smile. "Do you know what time it is?"

He looked at his watch. "Twenty-four past the hour."

"Wasn't this bus supposed to leave nine minutes ago?"

He shrugged and turned to stare out his window. "I suppose so."

I sat back down. Covering my face with my arm, I pretended to sleep. The engine vibrated below the backseat. I peeked up from the crook in my arm. The bus driver walked aboard and pulled the doors closed behind him, then sat down in the driver's seat.

"This is the nine fifteen to Chicago, with intermediate stops," he announced over the intercom. "Next stop, Wheeling, West Virginia." A safety instruction video began to play on the screens overhead.

After a long exhale of exhaust, the bus pulled out of the station. I peeked out the window. The grey Lexus was still there, and Alison and Detective Morris were headed toward another bus. My heart kept racing as we glided through the desolate streets of Alton. At every turn, I scanned the intersection for the grey Lexus. My ruse could have worked; they could be chasing the 9:30 to Boston. All they had to go on was the evidence I'd left, pointing them there.

Once we were out on the highway, I fought to relax. I was exhausted but unable to sleep. I remembered Alison's chilly voice: *"Nearing the Alaska site."* Hopefully I was moving away from it now. My head kept going in circles, trying to figure out what it meant, what Alaska even meant at all. Maybe it wasn't the place; maybe it was code, an acronym. I was sure I was missing something obvious.

I thought about that app they were working on so hard at MapOut: FYF, Find Your Friends. Harrison was hoping for millions in sales at Christmastime. Even before my dad died, I knew that what excited him about FYF—reuniting people—was different from what excited Harrison. FYF's primary function was to alert you anytime one of your digital contacts was within one mile of you. At first I loved the idea. How fun would it be to know where all your friends were at any given moment? But now it seemed creepy. No way would I want my "friends" to find me. And without my cell phone, they couldn't.

So, was "Alaska" code for something new, some kind of tracking or mapmaking app? A sophisticated mapping program Dad was working on in secret with Cleo? Did Harrison get angry because my dad wasn't sharing it with him? What could it stand for?

Then something else occurred to me. Harrison might have known I'd stumbled across my father's communications with Cleo. It seemed likely; no doubt a team of experts had torn that computer apart. So maybe he figured I'd try to find her. It wasn't that far of a leap to make. And he probably knew where she lived. No, definitely. The last time I saw Cleo, when Dad had gotten her that guest-teaching gig, Harrison had come to a dinner party at our house and tried to pick her up.

For a few months after that, Harrison kept referring to Cleo as the "hot little hippie." My dad would sort of laugh but I could tell he both was unnerved and annoyed. She was my dad's best friend from college. They'd met at MIT. But I think she was always more than that; she was my dad's Venus de Milo. I'm not saying my dad didn't fully and totally love my mom and Beth, but Cleo was the one he could never have. No one could have Cleo. She'd never married, never had children, never had a significant other in her life.

I could see what he saw in her: mystery. She lived off the grid, even though she'd been a better student than Dad and could have had her choice of jobs. (According to him, anyway.) She never talked about her past; she never mentioned her childhood or family. She traveled a lot, but it was never clear if it was for work or pleasure. Once I asked her what she did and she said, "Well, one of my passions is saving horses. I tend to them on my ranch." But I don't think anyone really knew.

No one except my dad.

Memories came and went as the bus sped north-northwest. I thought back to the last time Cleo's name had come up while he was alive: that phone call I'd remembered when Connor and I first hacked into my dad's computer.

I hadn't been able to sleep, so I went downstairs to have a snack. I could see through the stairwell window that the light was on in his shed. It was September; the nights were cool. I was wearing a long-sleeved T-shirt and sweat-pants, but my feet were bare; the grass tickled my toes. The window was cracked open.

Dad was talking on a grey flip-phone attached to a grey box four inches wide. His "special phone," as he called it. I never knew why it was special and I never asked. I thought it was a cell-phone-reception thing—our house was occasion-ally spotty—and figured it was a cool new gadget prototype, care of MapOut.

I hadn't planned on eavesdropping. I had planned on doing some kind of prank, like scraping my fingernails against the windowpane, like the vampires in *Salem's Lot*. So he'd shriek and we'd both laugh.

But he must have seen me outside.

He snapped his phone shut and asked me what I was doing.

"Looking for you," I'd said innocently.

In a way, I still was.

• • •

I spent the rest of the bus ride trying to decode the word *ALASKA*. I imagined Connor's finger in my palm, tracing letters. I tried to shove that daydream aside, but couldn't.

A is for Altitude

L is for Longitude

A is for Aerotriangulation

S is for Surveillance

K is for Kill-zone

A is for Access.

That was the first blind foray of dozens, maybe hundreds. The possibilities were endless (and ridiculous) but I couldn't stop my mind. For thirteen hours I tried; I tried and came up with nothing. How ironic: I needed an app for this.

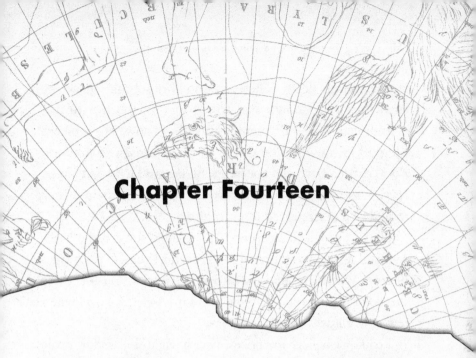

Chapter Fourteen

Union Station, Chicago, was the Alton train and bus depot's polar opposite: vast, crowded, and bustling, even at 11:28 P.M. I'd taken a taxi from the bus station to avoid surveillance cameras on mass transit. I only had a little over eighty dollars cash left. That was fine; I'd withdraw another three hundred at the stroke of midnight. I stared up at the Arrivals and Departures board. There was a Los Angeles–bound train with several stops in New Mexico, leaving at 12:05 A.M. That would cut it close—very close, but I had to risk it. And before then, I had to figure out how to buy the ticket without using my real name, which meant not showing ID.

My eyes roved over the atrium, never lingering on a person or group of people for longer than a second. I tried not to count the number of police and National Guardsmen. There was a huge food court, news shops, souvenir stores, and a café with Internet. I resisted the urge to run straight to the café. I kept reminding myself that it wasn't just risk;

it was certain death. There was no way I could check my email to see if Connor had tried to get in touch with me, even though it was all I could think about now. The moment I logged in, my location would be pinned in a few minutes. And I'd already vowed not to put Blaney and Rebs in danger. As sick as it made me feel, it would be best for them if they thought I'd disappeared forever, or worse.

First I needed to clean up. As I headed toward the bathrooms, I noticed that one of the souvenir shops sold Chicago Bears sweatshirts and sweatpants. Getting rid of these shredded jeans would help me blend in. Already, I'd caught a few long glances from some cops.

I couldn't believe the prices, twenty-eight dollars for a pair of black sweatpants. It would have to do. I decided to buy a new Bears baseball cap to match, so I looked like some diehard Chicago local. Thank God the cashier was too glued to his phone to notice the filthy waif in the Redskins cap who was shopping. He probably saw worse than me on a daily basis.

As I paid for the clothes, I smelled the stale stench of cigarettes. A man stood right behind me, a little too close in the line. He smiled at me when I turned around. He had short, ginger-colored hair, and wore a suit shirt and tie with a brown leather jacket. I don't know why exactly, there were lots of people in the store, but something about the way he smiled as though he knew me gave me the creeps.

I hurried across the station into the women's bathroom. Now I was down to forty-eight dollars. But as I washed up in the bathroom, I knew it was worth the money. I looked human again: clean from head to toe, with a matching cap and pants. Even the navy-blue sweatshirt didn't look so out of place.

After that, I stood in the line for the ticket window, mostly to kill time.

A few minutes later, a middle-aged woman with bright white teeth and brown hair in clips smiled at me.

"How can I help you?" she asked in a singsong voice.

"Um, how much is a one-way ticket to Elk, New Mexico? On the next train?"

The woman turned to her computer screen, typing slowly. I could see her fingers were knobby, her joints swollen. My grandmother had the same type of hands. I felt sorry for her, that behind her happy smile she must be in pain. I understood her, too.

"That would be train one seventy-five, leaving at twelve oh five P.M. . . . let's see." She stopped and squinted. "You'll have to transfer with a two-hour layover in Boyston. The fare is three hundred twenty-five dollars."

"Three hundred twenty-five dollars?" I repeated, before I realized how stupid I sounded.

"Yes, that's correct." She flashed a sympathetic smile. "If you had booked it two weeks in advance, the fare would have been two hundred and ten dollars."

I blinked. I wanted to answer, *"Well if I'd known two weeks ago that I would have been kidnapped from my office, drugged, and driven to Virginia to be murdered, then absolutely I would have booked the special discounted two-week advance fare."* Instead I forced a smile back at her. "Thanks for letting me know."

At 11:40, train number 175 was announced on the departures board. Track 11N. I scanned the station to find track 11N so

I would know where I'd have to run. It was 123 feet from the closest ATM machine to the gate. I positioned myself next to the machine so I could butt in front of someone if I had to at the right moment.

I started counting the minutes.

At exactly 12:01, I swiped my card. Punched in my password. I took one last glance around the huge station. No one seemed to be watching me, except for the fish-eye camera on the ATM. I felt my heart ticking like a bomb. The red pin on the map had dropped. Tanya Barrett was here. Even as I saw my new balance, $2,097.00, I wondered why Harrison hadn't frozen the account. He was my legal guardian, after all. Maybe he believed that if he kept me afloat, I would eventually come home. Or maybe he was keeping me out in the world for some reason.

I pressed WITHDRAW and punched in $300. I could hear the clicking sound as the machine counted out the bills in twenties.

As soon as I grabbed the money I bolted for the gate. My palms were sweating now. The card slipped from my hand, falling to the floor. Time was speeding up. My heart was racing. I didn't have time to pick up the card from the station floor. But that was fine. I didn't need it anymore, anyway. I had enough to get me to Elk, plus an extra $23 for food. My trail would go cold at Union Station, Chicago.

"Wait!" I called to the lone conductor on the empty platform. He held his hand on the door for me. I jumped on and he stepped in behind me. A loud bell rang and the door closed quickly behind us. I pressed the automatic door that led to the passenger car and collapsed into the nearest seat, sweaty and shaking, as the train pulled out of the station.

The midnight train wasn't crowded. After a few minutes, I moved closer to the center of the car and took a window seat. Harrison had probably already pinned me at Union Station ATM. But 400 trains left Union Station a day.

Good luck picking the right one.

"Tickets, please." The conductor's voice jolted me up.

"I don't have one. I have to buy one," I said, faking a yawn to disguise my strange behavior as fatigue.

"Reservation number?" He stared down at a rectangular black box in his hand, slightly larger than an iPhone.

"I didn't have time to make one. I'm sorry. This was a last-minute family emergency. I barely made the train."

He was tall, in his thirties, with brown hair and a nice, friendly face. There was a gold wedding ring on his finger.

"Okay, no reservation. Where are you heading?"

"Elk, New Mexico."

He took a book from his back pocket flipping through the thin phone book like pages. "Let's see . . . Elk, New Mexico. That'll be three hundred eighty dollars."

I shook my head. He must have got it wrong. "But I thought it was three hundred twenty-five?"

"If you buy on board, there's a penalty charge."

My throat felt thick. "I only have three hundred forty-eight." I reached into my pocket and shoved the wad of bills at him. "I'm so sorry. Can you help me out?"

He flipped back through his book of fares and destinations. "It's three hundred thirty if you get off the stop before, in Montgomery."

"Montgomery is one hundred forty-nine miles from Elk!" I cried.

The conductor raised his eyebrows, surprised. "You know your geography."

"Whatever, I'll take it," I said. My voice cracked, and I had to grit my teeth to hold back tears. It felt like the universe was conspiring against me in every way possible. Even Amtrak was against me. And I should have kept my mouth shut about geography.

"It's a two-day train journey. How are you going to eat or drink?"

I shrugged. "I don't know."

The conductor glanced over his shoulder, toward the front of the train. "Here," he said, handing me a receipt for Montgomery. He counted out change and placed the remaining eighteen dollars back in my hand. Then he took a pink slip and wrote *ELK* on it, and stuck it in the slot over my head. "Keep this with you at all times, and take it with when you transfer at Boyston," he said. "Café car's at the end, five cars down." He winked. "Go Bears!"

Now I couldn't hold back the tears. I managed a grateful laugh between sobs. I knew my face was turning red. I sniffed loudly.

"Thank you, sir," I stammered.

I lay down on the empty seat beside me, hoping the train would lull me to sleep. But when I closed my eyes, I could see the train moving through Chicago. I was watching it from above, like always. Every street was imprinted in my brain; I'd been to Chicago as a kid with my parents. I knew if this didn't stop, it would drive me crazy. I needed to sleep. I had pills for this, but they were in my medicine cabinet at home.

When I was younger, when I was helping my dad map the walking trails in the Amherst woods, I had the same sort of insomnia. At night, when I tried to sleep, my brain was tracking each step we took in the woods. From above, I could see all the trails, I could see my father and myself and everywhere we walked. After I was awake for two nights straight and verging on delirium, Dad took me to a doctor who prescribed me what Dad called "kiddie Ambien." I was eight and taking sleeping pills. I still took them sometimes, but I could control it better.

My dad credited the insomnia and compulsiveness to my gift, but it was one of those times that I didn't see it as a gift at all. Then, as now, it haunted me, like nightmares. Or more accurately: a waking alternative to nightmares.

I felt really, really alone staring at the dark window. I let myself think about Connor, about what he might be doing now. Right now. He was probably out somewhere with his girlfriend and Stanford friends. The last text he sent still made me miserable. I'd lost my phone but cruelly the text played inside my head.

"Sorry I didn't get to say bye in person . . . I might not be exactly where I want to be but I'll keep looking."

What did that mean exactly? Why even write that in a text? It was probably Connor's longest text ever. Maybe it was long because he felt so guilty over being such a cold-hearted person and terrible friend. Not to mention just stupid for spelling Piri Reis wrong.

Wait. There was no way Connor would have written such a long text, first of all. Second, after he wrote that my dad was such a big influence on him, he completely misquoted my dad's words. Then he spelled Piri Reis wrong. All of this wrapped up in a goodbye text?

Through the dark train windows the lights of the town we were passing by shone through the darkness. I felt freezing cold suddenly. Connor disappeared that night. The night we hacked into the emails. Harrison knew by the next morning and threatened me with criminal charges. Did he also threaten Connor? Did he punish him some other way? Did he force him back to California? Or worse, did he have someone kidnap him like they had done to me?

No. Harrison loved and adored Connor. He'd even given him a percentage of MapOut. No, I was just making up excuses for Connor. Making excuses, trying to find reasons why he could so easily just dump me as a friend. But it was still weird that he misspelled Piri Reis and even stranger that he misquoted my dad and that he talked about my dad at all in his text.

To change my thought process I focused again on the Alaska acronym I still hadn't uncovered. If Alaska was an acronym at all . . .

A is for Alison

L is for Lake

A is for Aptitude

S is for Snake

K is for Kettle

A is for Arsenic

I was delirious again, clearly. But exhaustion was able to take hold. Somewhere between Richmond and Harrington, I fell asleep.

• • •

It was noon the next day when I woke up. Fields spread out
for miles and miles and the sunlight was a gold color. I took
the Elk receipt and walked to the bathroom. I washed my
hands and face at the small sink. I tried to fix my hair as best
I could. Then I walked up the five cars to the café car.

I read the menu for a while, but for some reason I had no
appetite. I bought a can of Sprite and sat at one of the win-
dowed tables in the dining car.

A group of old ladies was playing gin rummy. They all
had southern accents; they jabbered at each other over a
large cooler of sandwiches and snacks. At another table sat
a family, a mother and father, a boy of about twelve and his
teenage sister. The parents were texting on their cell phones
and the boy was playing Subway Surfers on his iPad. The
teenage girl wore black eyeliner and glared out the window
with her headphones on, a sour look on her face.

Lucky girl. As miserable as she was, she still had both parents and a brother.

I suddenly realized why I wasn't hungry. It was because I
felt a sickening dread. What if Harrison had already gotten
to Cleo?

"Remind you of your family?" a voice asked.

I jerked up to see a strange man smiling down at me. He
was wearing a white button-down shirt and tie with a brown
faded leather jacket. I instantly placed him; this was the same
paunchy middle-aged guy I'd seen in the souvenir shop back
at Union Station.

"I'm sorry. I didn't mean to scare you. I travel alone a lot
for business and I sometimes find myself staring, too. Staring

at families that remind me of my own, when I'm feeling especially homesick."

I shook my head, my mind whirling too fast for a response. This guy must have been following me. Which meant he must have been sent by Harrison. His ill-fitting suit smelled of stale cigarettes. Could he be the smoker who'd been with Alison?

His smile faltered. It went from apologetic, to confused, to something else. "I'll leave you alone," he said, hurrying off to get in line for food.

I ran back to my seat, lurching through the train cars and spilling my soda as I went. I switched cars, and then switched cars again. And then I waited for the man.

At 7:00 P.M., hunger finally compelled me to return to the café car. The man was nowhere to be found—at least that I could see. I spent ten dollars as carefully as I could: the most food for the least amount of money. Chips, fruit, granola bars. No more beverages; I'd drink water from the little cone cups. As I returned to my seat, I saw the man sleeping, his hands on his lap. I headed to the very last car on the train.

The next thirty-six hours were a blur of panic and hunger. But at three A.M. in Boyston, where I transferred to a new train, I made sure to pass by the man with the tie and leather jacket on my way out. He was on his cell phone, but he didn't exit. His eyes met mine as I did. The kind conductor who'd saved me nodded as I exited. I wanted to hug him, to thank him, to get his name so I could somehow repay him, but I just waved.

The train pulled away, I clutched my ticket and phony receipt, hoping it would get me there.

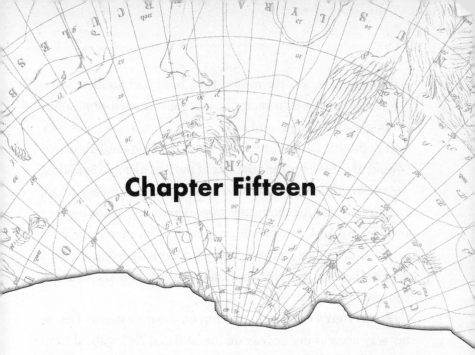

Chapter Fifteen

The last two hours between Montgomery and Elk were the longest in my life. At ten o'clock in the morning, I stepped off the train. The sun felt warm against my skin, and the air smelled like grass and sand. Only two other people exited with me: a couple in their forties. I took off my sweatshirt and tied it around my waist. My undershirt felt sticky. I followed the couple around the train station—little more than a red clapboard shack—to the two-lane highway in front.

The hot sun glared off the sparkles in the asphalt road. The road was flat and long, running due east and west, parallel to the train tracks. The desert spread out on toward distant mountains on both sides, dotted with scrub brush and cactuses.

My ankle was sore again. What was I supposed to do now? From the east, I heard the loud roar of a motor. A moment later, a jeep appeared. A wild-looking, grey-haired woman in a bright sundress skidded up, and in hopped the couple. I was half tempted to ask them for a ride, but I had no idea where I was going. The jeep sped off, leaving the smell of gasoline mixing with the sand and sun.

My mouth felt dry. I hadn't been drinking enough water. Would my ankle hurt for the rest of my life, always reminding me of this time? I had to erase that thought from my mind; I couldn't think of the future now. There might not even be one. I'd banked everything on finding Cleo here, and that might not happen. I needed to sit down; I needed water. I stared ahead at the desolate line of road, and then turned back to the station.

A furry grey cat slept in the sun on the doorstep as I made my way up, leaning heavily on the banister. As I walked from the bright sunlight into the shade, I suddenly felt dizzy. The station was little more than a single room cluttered with old junk, manned by one attendant, an old man with a shock of white hair who sat in a booth. A battered schedule hung from the wall facing him, surrounded by framed black-and-white photos of cowboys and desert scenes. A box of Astro Pops sat beside the man at his post, along with a cash register. Next to the booth stood a side table with the white pages and an old-fashioned, clunky rotary phone. The whole place looked like it was from another era.

"You okay, miss?" he asked.

"Just thirsty," I said.

He pointed to the bench under the schedule. Beside it sat a metal bucket of ice with bottled water. I took one of the bottles and started chugging.

"You wouldn't happen to sell aspirin?" I gasped, once I'd drained nearly half the bottle. "Or ace bandages?"

He reached into a drawer, taking a bottle of aspirin. He poured two out in the palm of his hand and extended out the booth window. It took me a moment to figure out he was giving them to me.

"Thanks." I washed them down. "How much for the water?"

"On the house. No ace bandage though."

There was no way I could make it any distance on my ankle. "Is there a cab service around here?"

"There's a guy in Jackson," the man said.

It didn't sound promising. "Can I use your phone? I'll pay."

He grinned, as if he'd heard this question a million times from out-of-towners like me. "Sure, but don't talk for too long."

The white pages were labeled ELK, JACKSON, RHINE, and CANE COUNTIES. They were half an inch thick. I flipped to the letter W for Wright.

I ran my finger down the names.

Mr. and Mrs. Allen Wright

Brett Wright

C. Wright 725-445-3897

The number looked familiar, but I couldn't be sure. I knew I needed it to be hers, so my mind could be deceiving me. I picked up the receiver. My hands were sweaty. I put my finger in four, pulling the dial around and letting it go. The only other time I'd ever used a rotary phone was at Beth's grandmother's house. It didn't work. I'd tried it just for fun. Now I pressed the heavy handset to my ear, listening to the faraway sound of the ring. I had a hopeless, sinking feeling that she wouldn't pick up.

"Hello?"

Cleo. I took a sharp breath in, stunned. "Cleo. It's Tanya. Don't hang up."

There was silence on her end.

"Cleo, please." I blinked and realized tears were streaming down my face. Relief that she had answered the phone turned to fear that she would refuse to speak to me, that she would hang up on me like before. "I'm begging you—"

"Tanya, just tell me where you are."

I took in a gulp of air. "I'm at the Elk train station . . ."

"Hang up the phone and don't move. I'll be there in twenty minutes."

I did as she said. The receiver felt as heavy as an anchor in my hand as I placed it back on the hook. I gave the man a dollar bill, the last I had, for the call. He asked me something as I left, but I was still in shock, too dazed to hear his words or respond as I stepped outside. The door swung shut behind me. I sat down on the steps next to the sleeping cat. The air was still and hot. I held my ankle where it throbbed.

The cat stood and stretched, then nuzzled against me. I rubbed her soft grey fur and stared out at the empty highway. Another tear fell from my cheek. Did she remind me of Bootsy? I couldn't tell. A secret part of me wondered if I'd already died, if I'd reunited with my dead pet at some bizarre weigh station on the way to the afterlife.

I wasn't sure how much time had passed, five minutes, twenty, an hour, when I heard the distant purr of an engine. The speck that appeared in the distance became a forest-green Range Rover speeding toward me. It pulled up in front of the station, and there she was: a vision with that wild blonde-streaked mane and that freckled face I remembered so clearly, shaded by round brown sunglasses and a cowboy hat. The radio blasted some old classic rock song; it was one my father loved, about a woman named Maggie.

"Get in," Cleo commanded over the music.

I hesitated, but then she flashed a smile. It was wide and easygoing, with a little trace of impishness, just as I remembered, too. Her tanned, toned arms gripped the steering wheel. She had on a white tank top and a silver chain with a turquoise star. I stared as I limped toward her, not because I realized then that she was one of the most gorgeous women I'd ever seen—something that had always eluded me about her before—but because I still couldn't believe she was really here, in front of me, waiting.

There were so many questions I wanted to ask.

"I am so happy you did what I'd hoped you'd do," Cleo murmured before I could utter a word. I crawled in beside her, slamming the door. She lifted her sunglasses and her nose wrinkled. A look of worry set in her eyes. "I want to hear it all. I'll feed you, too. And I'll get you in the shower first thing."

"Cleo . . ." I started to speak.

"Shush." She took me in her arms, holding me to her. I felt myself sigh, and the sigh turned to tears. "You're gonna be okay," she whispered.

Her eyes went to a flat computer screen on her lap, glowing purple. It was about the size of an iPad but four inches thicker. She held her finger over her lip and I knew not to say another word. I looked behind me, but no one was there.

"Buckle up." She clasped the wheel, cranking the radio.

The car went from zero to forty to seventy. The wind whipped my hair straight out behind me. The Bears hat flew off my head and tumbled back behind us, down the desolate road. She put the computer on my lap.

"Raise your hand if you see orange or red."

"It's just purple now," I yelled over the wind and music. I gripped the handle, forcing a smile, even though I felt queasy. I didn't want Cleo to see me weak, or know that I was afraid of being in a speeding car. Finally, after ten-plus miles, she slowed a little so I wouldn't have to shout over the wind and music.

"Now tell me what happened," she said. "But remember if you see orange or red, stop talking."

I took a deep breath. "So what happened was I had a summer job working at MapOut with Harrison's son, Connor. One night we broke into my dad's computer to look at his emails. He had three security gates set up but I figured out his code."

Cleo smiled. "Good work."

"But the next day, Connor wasn't at work. Harrison found out what we'd done and threatened me. He told me Connor had decided to suddenly go back to Stanford."

Her eyes flashed to the computer screen, then back to the road. "Did you hear from Connor again?"

"Just one weird text saying what his dad said, minus the Stanford part. I guess MapOut is going west, too."

"And it was weird, you say? Weird how?"

"The way it was written, it was off. It was . . ." That word floated back through the recesses of my memory, the word Beth had used, the word that had come back to me in the coffee shop while waiting for a boy I'd never see again. "Unhinged."

Cleo nodded. "Okay, we'll come back to that." She chewed her lip, staring out at the highway. "What else?"

The rest tumbled out in a confused jumble: the last night at MapOut, Alison and the men who drugged me; Harrison saying "Alaska" over the computer; finding my way to her. I checked the computer screen. Still purple.

"What's Alaska?" I asked, once I could catch my breath. Cleo hadn't interrupted once. "What's it code for?"

"It's not code."

"Oh." I swallowed. My face felt hot even with the wind blasting. I wasn't sure if I were embarrassed or just frustrated. How many miles had I spent trying to decode it? On the other hand, those hundreds of meaningless acronyms probably saved what was left of my sanity. I would have succumbed to panic if I hadn't kept occupied. I would have probably attacked that creepy guy with the leather jacket, even though that's probably all he was: a creepy guy with a leather jacket.

"Your dad discovered a 'black spot' in Alaska," Cleo explained. "A place that doesn't appear on any maps or any satellite imagery. There's a reason it can't be mapped, and that's what your dad was trying to figure out."

"I thought he was working on something in Cambodia. I thought, you know, that's why he had to go there. On the work trip when he died."

"Cambodia?" She flashed a bitter smile. "That was all a smoke screen, a lie. Tanya, he never even went there for work. He disappeared. The same way you would have disappeared if you hadn't escaped."

The blue sky and grey road blurred together. My vision

felt as if it were dimming. Something rose in my throat. "Can you slow down, please?"

"Sorry, sweetie, of course."

Cleo eased back on the gas. For a moment I thought I was going to be sick, but the nausea passed, leaving something less than emptiness. It was the same hollow, numb sensation I'd felt when I first heard the news of his death. It was worse. It was as if he'd died all over again, just now. I stared out at the flat desert. *How had they killed him? Was it Alison or the smoker? Did they shoot him point-blank? Did he beg for his life? Did he think about me?* I squeezed my eyes shut.

I felt Cleo's hand on my shoulder.

"Why did you take my call this time?" I breathed. "I mean, why didn't you take it when I called you last week?"

She hugged me close as she drove. "You called from MapOut last week. This week, you called from my local train station. Big difference. Not to mention, there's an APB out for your arrest."

"Right. Harrison." I spat the word. "He's behind all of this, isn't he? He's the one who wanted my dad dead."

Cleo shrugged, placing both hands back on the wheel. "I'm not so sure it's that simple. There was a time in his life when Harrison loved your dad. I don't think he's calling the shots. I think they have him by the balls. They have something he wants or needs and he's their puppet."

"Who are *they*?" I asked, baffled.

"That's what your dad and I were trying to find out, sweetie."

Something didn't fit. I couldn't bring myself to believe that Harrison was just someone else's stooge. He was too smart, too cunning. "Do you know if my dad and Harrison ever fought over anything?" I asked. "I mean, did he tell you?"

She flashed a brief, sad smile. "Boots."

I frowned. "What?"

"The winter before last, Harrison bought the exact same kind of hiking boots as your dad. I don't know why, but your dad lost it. That was when your dad and I really started digging. I'd never heard him so pissed off. It was like the final straw, working with this slick guy who slipped on a different personality to suit whatever occasion. He wanted the new investors to think he and Michael were peas in a pod, these rugged outdoorsmen, like he was just as passionate as Michael about mapping the land with his own eyes . . ."

I'd stopped listening. *Boots.*

It all came flooding back. I saw a bird's-eye view of a trail of boot prints in the snow behind our house. Rage flashed through me, rage at Harrison for fooling me into forgetting that my father was dead that awful winter's day. It was Harrison who'd snuck onto our property, Harrison who'd broken into my dad's shed looking for something, Harrison who'd played that cruel trick. Of course it was.

Cleo slowed the car, turning south off the highway onto a gravel road. The sun was high overhead. "Tanya, what is it?"

"Just trying to figure things out," I said, my jaw clenched.

"Tell me about the email that Connor sent. The weird one."

I recited it word for word; I knew it by heart. "'Sorry I didn't get a chance to say bye in person. Going back to California was a last-minute decision. MapOut needs a West Coast office space and they needed me to find it. I might not be exactly where I want to be but I'll keep looking. Your dad was an inspiration to me the way Perry Reese was to him. I know you understand. Hope the rest of your summer goes well.'"

Cleo nodded. "What struck you as weird?"

"All of it. He spelled Piri Reis wrong, for starters. And the thing about not being exactly where he wanted to be—he made this huge point of telling me on my first day at MapOut that he would make sure he'd be exactly where he wanted to be for the rest of his life, because my dad inspired him. Which was why he wanted to go to Tanzania, *not* California. Which I would have known. The whole thing . . . it was just *fake*."

"Yup. I agree," Cleo said without missing a beat.

I glanced at her. My hand gripped the armrest as we bumped along the increasingly rough road. "You do?"

"Connor isn't in California. He's being held against his will. His captors told him to contact you, either to assuage your concerns or to suss you out, or both. He was clever enough to send a hidden message. My guess is that he knows what happened to your father now, too. It's all in there: he's not where he wants to be, and something is wrong."

For some reason, I wanted to hug her. Where was this freakish hope and happiness coming from? This was the worst possible news. But then it occurred to me: I'd first suspected as much. Connor wasn't a creep. Connor was a victim, like me. And something else also hit me then, too: Harrison *was* too smart to be a stooge. And too strong. Whoever "they" were, they couldn't influence or control him with money. For all of Harrison's middle-aged, Porsche-driving, Armani-suited, second-tier model-dating persona, the one real thing in his life was his love for Connor. That was their weapon.

"I think that they frightened Harrison when they killed your dad," Cleo continued as if reading my mind. "But it wasn't enough. They needed to find his Achilles' heel."

"Connor," I breathed.

"So, did you text him back?"

I nodded, more ashamed than ever of what I'd written. "I pretty much told him to screw off."

"Then the kidnappers showed up?" Cleo asked.

"Yeah. Fifteen minutes later."

She whistled and her lips curved downward. "You are a very brave girl, you know that? But right then, you let them know your position. You were expendable at that point and a confirmed threat. My guess is that they wanted to interrogate you at a secure location, just to make sure exactly what you knew, and then dispose of you. I'm sure they were planning to use that as more ammunition against Harrison, too."

Dispose of me? The words left me numb. In Cleo's world this probably happened all the time . . . People were disposed of, like garbage.

I didn't want her to see my face as I turned away. What had I gotten into? My hands felt cold. I squeezed my eyes shut. I wished I could just be whisked away to my home, my *true* home. I wanted to be in my room with Bootsy, my mom downstairs in the kitchen, my dad in his office. I wanted to go back in time and stay there.

Cleo spun left off the gravel onto a dirt road, where a group of houses were clustered together around a communal vegetable garden. Sunburned half-naked children played between the houses. Chickens roamed inside a large coop; wet laundry hung from yards of clothesline. Fifty feet of southward-facing solar panels reflected the noonday sun. Her house was the last one in the cul-de-sac: white clay with a red-tiled terra-cotta roof.

We jerked to a stop. She rushed around to my side to help me out.

Two large mutts greeted us with barks and wagging tails.

"Good boys," Cleo cooed as they followed us into the house.

It felt cool inside. I slumped down at the kitchen table, while Cleo heated up a pot of soup on the stove. She stepped outside to pour me a glass of water from a pump well. It tasted so pure, so clean. Back in the kitchen, she took a small brown bottle from the shelf.

"Stick out your tongue," she said.

"What is it?"

"Arnica. It'll help the swelling."

The drops tasted like alcohol. She told me to prop my foot up on a chair, then wrapped an ice pack around my swollen ankle. The smell of chicken soup filled the kitchen. She poured me a large bowl and carried it over to me. It was steaming hot, full of carrots, potatoes, and kale. After the ice-cold water and the bitter medicine, the hot liquid going down my throat was the best thing ever.

"Did you make this?"

Cleo sneered. "No, I ordered it from FreshDirect."

"What I meant was . . . Is this one of your chickens? In the soup?

"What do you think, they're just pets? Get real, honey."

I almost smiled. This was the Cleo I knew, the Cleo my dad had fallen in love with—not in a physical way, in a familial way, an eternal way. A thousand more questions gnawed at my brain, but I ignored them for now. I wanted to savor this feeling I'd forgotten, this feeling of being me, of being safe.

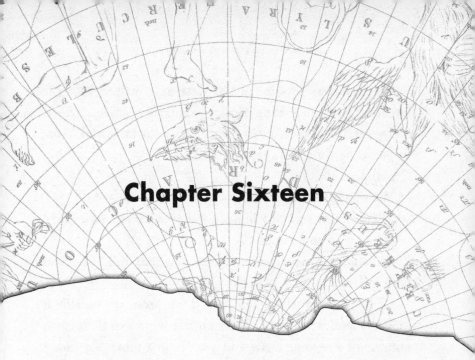

Chapter Sixteen

After the soup was gone, I took a long nap in a spare bedroom with daisy-print sheets. Then Cleo led me to her outdoor
shower, made of cedar wood. I grasped the metal pulley and
hot water poured over me. I lathered up with soap, washed my
hair twice and rinsed. I felt a thousand times better. Back in the
bedroom, Cleo had laid out some clean clothes. A pair of jeans,
underwear, and a faded pale green sweatshirt of hers. They fit
me, sort of; she was just a little taller so I rolled up the cuffs and
sleeves. I never wanted to see the Alton sweatshirt again.

There was something else on the bed: a silver gun. Did she
mean to leave it for me? I looked around the room, noticing
something else. There were pictures, family pictures, but Cleo
wasn't in any of them. A diploma hung on the wall, not from
MIT where Cleo had gone to school with my dad. The diploma
was from the University of New Mexico and the name on it was
Patricia Jones.

What was Cleo hiding? Who was she hiding from?

The sun was sinking in the west as I walked into the kitchen. Cleo was feeding her dogs a mixture of rice, carrots, and vegetables. I took a pen from a jar on the table and wrote in the corner of a newspaper.

Can we talk?

She shook her head. "How's your ankle feeling?"

"Better, sort of." She handed me another ice pack and I wrapped it around my ankle.

"I want to introduce you to my neighbor Bill," she said with a wink.

Cleo led me to the house next door. From the outside it looked identical to hers. Through the windows I caught a glimpse of a reading chair and a lamp on a table. She didn't knock or turn the handle on the door. Beneath the window box was a pad; she pressed a series of numbers, and the door opened. The first thing I noticed was the sound, the hum of generators. There was no reading chair, no lamp. The window projected a false image.

In the spare windowless chamber, Cleo sat down in front a large-screen computer. Her fingers moved quickly over the keypad, typing in a series of codes. I sat down on a stool beside her. The smell in the room reminded me of being inside an airplane cabin. Soundproofing material covered the ceiling and walls. An image appeared on the screen: glaciers and rocks. It was a home video; you could hear the sound of footsteps and see the movement of the camera, and then I heard my dad's voice off screen. It was the first time I'd heard the sound of his voice since he died.

I stared, mesmerized, holding my breath.

"This is what your dad found," Cleo said.

"I don't get it. Is it Alaska?"

"Yes. But it doesn't exist on any satellite imagery or maps. The only way to see it is to physically be there."

"Maybe it's so remote that Google Maps hasn't bothered to get to it yet. I mean, it's not exactly Times Square."

Cleo clicked on a second image. Denali National Park, a scene from satellite imagery. She zoomed, uncovering the whole landscape. "See what happens here?"

"Nothing," I said.

"Right. It's been erased."

I examined the image of grey-and-blue topography. "Let me see that," I said. I took the keyboard and googled maps of Denali National Park. It was founded in 1917. I studied the earliest maps. I then superimposed the most defined satellite imagery over it, starting in 1960, 1965, 1970, 1975, 1980, 1985, 1990, 1995, 2000, 2001, 2002 . . .

I thought of Piri Reis. Maybe it was hearing my dad's voice. "Can you pull up the satellite image and superimpose it over this map?"

Cleo took the keyboard and pulled up the satellite imagery, then dropped the map from 1940 over it. The place my father found existed in 1940, but not today. I rolled over the topography in 1940 to 1986. Everything matched up.

"Okay, let's get the satellite view from 1987 to today." Was this a place so remote it had been forgotten? Impossible. Had the climate changed so drastically in the last twenty years it had disappeared into the water, and then resurfaced? Highly unlikely. From 1917 to 1987, the place my father found was clearly marked on the map: a five-mile-by-seven-mile swath of land. There was nothing particularly outstanding about the topography, nothing that I could make out. I squinted, practically putting my nose to the screen, examining every rock, every tree.

"Sweetie, you'll ruin your eyes. Lemme help you." Cleo took the keyboard from me. "Try this one."

What appeared on the screen was a perfectly defined, moving image of Denali National Park. Red spots appeared dotted around the glaciers. I knew what they were: body heat from animals and the human visitors.

I turned to Cleo, finally asking the one question that had been burning inside me since she'd picked me up at the train station. "What do you do?"

She shrugged.

"I mean, who do you work for? The government?"

Cleo cocked her head. "Maybe I do. Maybe I don't. Maybe I did. Maybe I didn't."

"Right," I said, staring back at the screen. I knew I wouldn't get a straight answer, and I also knew that it was possibly for my own protection.

"Zoom in on the stream," I said. I felt my heart racing. The image was crystal clear. In the stream, a splash of red salmon swam upstream, north to south. I followed the river on the computer until the black spot, where it disappeared. What was happening? I traveled backward again, knowing I'd missed something. I watched it again, and again. Thirty times, following the bend of the stream.

"Do you see what I see?" I said to Cleo.

Cleo nodded slowly. "The river was gone. The water slowed to a pool. Someone had redirected the water flow. Built a dam and changed the water pathway."

"But why would someone redirect it and then make the place disappear?"

"Water and oxygen. The two main staples of life on Earth. Science 101."

"Right. Science 101."

I touched the image of the stream on the computer, following it to where it disappeared, to the "black spot" as she'd called it.

"How can I get there?" I asked.

"Sweetheart, you're not going anywhere. You're not risking your life for this. They'll squash you without a second thought and no one will know. They'll cover their tracks just like they did when they killed your father."

The reality of her words fell against me. I felt hopeless, insignificant.

"They can't just keep killing people and getting away with it," I insisted as her eyes flickered over my face. "Someone will investigate. Someone will find out." I was talking loudly, furiously. The injustice of it was burning inside of me. They killed my dad without leaving a trace? Without any consequences? They couldn't keep getting away with it.

"Ever taken a history class, sweetheart?" Cleo asked. "Or do the schools just give you PG versions of the truth? The powerful get away with mass murder all the time. Countries, corporations, individuals . . . It's nice to see you're an idealist but let's get back to the facts."

"I'm going with or without your help."

Cleo laughed. "Good luck getting the visitors' bus to take you. And don't forget your mosquito clothes and pepper spray to keep the grizzlies away."

"Cleo, please—"

"End of discussion," she interrupted, her smile gone. "I have some work to finish up here, private work. Go back to my house and make yourself at home. You can't get into any trouble there, unless you play with guns."

Cleo stayed at "Bill's house" until nightfall. She had a tele-scope on a tripod at her living room window, next to a side table and sofa. When she returned, I began looking through it at the clear sparkling stars, at the glow of the crescent moon. I doubted it was the stars Cleo was looking for in the night sky.

In the kitchen she cooked up a stir-fry from vegetables in her garden. I got bored of the telescope and picked up a black-and-white photo of Cleo and a family. It probably wasn't even hers. The picture wasn't recent. Cleo looked about twelve years old.

"Did you ever go to the place in Alaska with Dad?" I asked.

Cleo froze. She had her back to me but I could see the question made her nervous. "That was my camera," she said. "As soon as we found the house, we knew that it wasn't left off the maps by mistake. It was no accident."

"The house?"

"Later, Tanya." She turned off the stove and carried two steaming plates to the table. "You need to eat something."

"What house?" I persisted.

She leaned back and sighed, then waved me outside into the backyard. She began walking into the desert. I followed.

"You're just as stubborn as your dad, you know that?" she said. "There was a cabin. We thought it belonged to the park ranger. We didn't see anyone. Your dad filmed it. Then we went back to the campsite. We had something to eat, and he went to catch a plane back home. That was the last time I saw him."

I swallowed. "He never got on the plane. He never came back home."

"No, he disappeared somewhere before he reached the airport. There were no witnesses I could find. Nothing on surveillance in Alaska. The thing was, they didn't know I was with him. They didn't know I had already downloaded a copy of the video. When I got back to civilization, the Cambodia story was in full swing—" She broke off. "Tanya, he only told you that he went to Cambodia to protect you and Beth. That was his story."

I ignored the lump in my throat. I had to focus on what was going on here, now. My dad was dead, but if what Cleo was saying were true, if her hunch was correct, then Connor was still alive and his life hung in the balance—over *this*.

"So all this has something to do with the house? Is it the government?"

"No," she said firmly. "Not unless it's a security division I can't access. But that's unlikely."

"Cleo, you have to help me get there. I need to find out what happened to him."

"That's what the police are for," she said. "That's what the government is for, too. Trust me. You're safe here, and that's what matters."

"Harrison and the rest of MapOut say he drowned in Cambodia. And you know that. They even have his plane ticket to prove he was there. They even have him on tape, leaving the airport and checking into his hotel."

Cleo raised an eyebrow. "Have you seen the tape? It's not exactly high definition, is it, sweetheart? It's a black-and-white blur of a white man in his late forties."

"You mean . . . ?"

"I mean, whoever is behind this has a lot of money, resources, and has their asses covered."

"I still need to try. It's not just about my dad. It's about Connor, too. It's my fault he was even snooping—"

"Okay. okay." Cleo held up her hand, stopping me. "I understand what you want to do. Go in and eat something before it gets cold. I'm going back to Bill's."

Half an hour later, after I'd cleaned my plate and returned to the telescope, Cleo came back inside. She held a metal brief-case that she set on the table. She opened the top; inside was a collection of small pistols. I couldn't take my eyes off them. They filled me with a sense of fear and dread I wasn't pre-pared for. I wasn't ready to shoot anyone.

"I don't . . . I don't know how to use a gun," I stammered. Nor did I want to.

"You might need to learn. Or you can take the laser."

She pulled out what looked like a harmonica box. Inside was a thin silver tube, with an electronic screen on the side.

"This is simple to use. It won't kill anyone, but it will knock them out temporarily."

I let out a breath. "Okay."

"I'll show you how to use it. You touch the screen with your thumb. It will imprint your fingerprints. No one else

will be able to use it, even if they take it from you. It's undetectable, too, or as close to undetectable as you can get." She
handed it to me.

"Thank you, Cleo." I felt cold with fear as I turned it
around in my hand. It was oddly heavy, as if it were made of
lead or gold. I knew this was what I had to do, but somehow
the reality of it hadn't quite set in.

"Let's get ready. Gretchen will be here soon."

"Who's Gretchen?"

"She works with me." I could tell by the finality of her tone
that this was probably all she'd offer in terms of explanation.
"By the way, we're coming with you. Your dad would kill me
if he knew what I was letting you do, but I know you'll try to
get there, anyway."

I forced a smile, even though I was so anxious I could
barely speak. Cleo took me into her bedroom. She opened
her closet revealing an array of jeans, T-shirts, and sweaters.
Then she took a key from the top shelf, unlocking a second
door hidden behind the hanging clothes. She pulled out
unopened clear bags; inside were plain grey jackets, pants,
and sweaters.

"There's lead inside the fibers; no one will be able to detect
weapons beneath."

I pulled the jacket on; it felt the same as any other jacket,
just slightly heavier and the material stiffer. She gave me
warm socks and a pair of boots to wear, too. "It's cold there,
even in the summer."

Cleo filled the dogs' bowls with fresh water and gave them
each an extra few handfuls of food.

"Goodbye my sweeties, I'll be back soon. Rita will take

good care of you." The dogs whimpered, knowing she was leaving.

I heard a strange sound, almost like a propeller plane. It hummed overhead, and then its pitch dropped. It popped, crackled, and faded into silence. It was past midnight. Cleo scrawled a note to her neighbor, asking her to feed the dogs and horses while she was gone. We went outside, where she slipped the note under her neighbor's door. I looked back at the house, the two dogs were watching through the window as we walked across the desert. I caught a whiff of gasoline, and in the moonlight I could just make out a silhouette of a tiny propeller plane. A woman stood beside it.

"That's Gretchen," Cleo said.

My heart seized. I wasn't generally afraid of flying—but this crazy-looking woman didn't seem much older than me. Her light brown hair was cut short in a boyish style, and she had a diamond stud in her nose. She wore a leather bomber jacket.

"Gretchen, meet Tanya," Cleo said as she gave Gretchen a huge hug.

I hesitated.

"Sweetheart, Gretchen is a pilot for some very important people."

"Come on, get in," Gretchen urged, holding out a hand and opening the door for me. "Flying is the safest way to travel. We're already about twenty minutes behind schedule and we need to do this in the dark."

Swallowing my fear, I took her hand and clambered aboard.

Cleo sat up front next to Gretchen and I ducked into the

third seat in the back. I fastened my seat belt and closed my eyes as the propellers started up. The plane roared across the desert. It wasn't until we were off the ground that I realized we were flying in the dark. Literally. There were no lights on the plane; the only light came from the instrument panel. We were black against the night sky.

We rose up and up for about ten minutes or so. The flight seemed smooth, or at least as smooth as a propeller plane can be. I felt the tension in my stomach ease for a moment when Gretchen suddenly nose-dived fifty feet before settling the plane again. I covered my hand with my mouth.

"I think she's gonna be sick," Gretchen alerted Cleo.

Cleo rummaged around the front of the plane and handed back a white wax-paper bag. I grabbed it but I wasn't sick. I think I was actually too nervous to throw up, even though I wanted to.

"I know it's not the smoothest flight," Gretchen shouted from the front. "But it's better than being shot down."

"We're avoiding detection," Cleo stated more clearly.

"Yeah, I got that."

I squeezed my eyes shut and covered my ears with my hands.

Chapter Seventeen

The air smelled like ice as we landed on the barren tundra. The sound of the slowing propellers faded into the wind that blew westward, sending blasts of snow tumbling across the flat expanse of white. We'd been aloft for over twelve hours. Gretchen cut the engine and pulled on a coat and gloves. She took something that looked like a metal briefcase from beneath the pilot's seat.

"You have the box?" Cleo spoke in a whisper.

Gretchen nodded. In the creeping dawn I could see her profile, short brown hair, clear skin; from the side she almost looked like a boy. Cleo pulled her own hair back, twisting it into a bun at the base of her neck.

"What are we waiting for?" I leaned forward.

Cleo looked at Gretchen for an answer. Gretchen monitored the screen; it was purple except for four tiny dots of red, flickering like flames. "I don't know if they are human or animal."

"They look human to me," Cleo said, and for the first time I detected a nervousness in her voice. "If they were animals they would be in a pack or farther apart."

"They can't see us in here," Gretchen said.

Gretchen and Cleo watched the moving infrared dots on the screen. Outside, I could make out the shadows of huge trees and land around us in the early dawn light.

"Someone's coming close." Gretchen pulled out a gun, gripping it in her hand. We looked out at the darkness, completely silent in the cabin.

The reflection of two sets of eyes appeared in the dim blue morning light: wolves. They circled the body of the plane not with fear just with curiosity. They sniffed around, but the cold metal scent didn't interest them and they moved on, disappearing into the woods, leaving no trace but a red trail on the screen.

"It's clear," Cleo said, gesturing to the screen. "Darkness is our best cover."

"Okay." I was growing increasingly nervous. What had I thought, that I'd be coming here to map the park? Observe the wildlife? Yes, that's what I had thought, sort of, or wanted to think. Cleo showed me how to strap the weapon to the inside of my arm, where it lay flush against my skin, hidden beneath my sleeve.

Outside, it was freezing. My cheeks burned; I could see icy blasts of my own breath. Gretchen was going to stay by the plane. Cleo placed a small compass in my hand. I didn't need it, but I took it, anyway. The sun was starting to appear above the horizon; cautiously I started east with Cleo by my side.

On the long flight, Gretchen had warned me not to speak while we were outside. The coats Cleo had given us would hide our body heat from infrared detection, make us invisible. Then again, this entire place was invisible—

A roaring ball of fire shot through the trees.

"Cleo!" I screamed.

An explosion drowned out my voice. Flames burst from seemingly everywhere around me. The air was suddenly thick with black smoke. In that instant, I lost my bearings. I had no sense of direction. I couldn't see Cleo; I couldn't see the plane. I tried to make my way through the thick smoke but it was impossible. I couldn't breathe.

"Cleo!" I shouted again as another ball of fire exploded nearby.

"Go!" Cleo shouted.

I felt the searing heat, very close now, and panic took hold. I ran blindly, trying to outrun the smoke. I looked behind me; I couldn't see Cleo. I didn't stop running. I knew the smoke would suffocate me. I ran until I fell from exhaustion. My lungs were tight. I choked for air on my hands and knees, covering my mouth with my shirt, trying to breathe.

As the smoke cleared, I found myself in the woods. I had lost Cleo and Gretchen completely. I was sure they would find me, that I would see her at the "place." She and Gretchen were prepared for this. They'd been expecting it. That's what I told myself as I tried to stand, and see through the clearing smoke.

"Cleo? Gretchen?" I shouted their names.

No answer. *Please have made it back to the plane, please be safe.* But another part of me made a grim tally. Again, I'd put someone in danger. Two people. Cleo had warned me not to come and I'd insisted. As I ran ahead frantically searching for them, I knew she'd been right. I was lost, alone in the woods in Alaska. But Cleo was alive, at least. She'd yelled at me to run. Maybe she was searching for me. Even in the plane they wouldn't see me in the woods. I had to get somewhere where I might be visible from the sky.

The woods could stretch for hundreds of miles. The smoke was so thick, so heavy, and it lingered. I couldn't see to orient myself with the sun. I felt my belt; I had the weapon Cleo had given me and my compass. I took out my compass but could barely see the needle . . .

My ears perked up. The birds had cleared out with the explosion, and the woods were all but silent—except for the sound of rushing water. I stiffened, listening. *The river,* I thought, *the river we had seen on the satellite images*. I knew where it would lead if the images were accurate.

I crawled toward the sound, trying to stay below the toxic cloud of smoke. But when I reached the riverbank, my heart sank. The river was over fifteen feet wide, rushing powerfully downstream from the mountains. Chunks of ice from the glaciers floated in the strong current. On the maps it was a meek stream. In my father's video, it was slow moving, almost still.

I cupped my hands, washing the soot from my face and gulping down handfuls of water. The icy liquid soothed my parched throat. I glanced around, wiping my mouth. Where was the small house my father had found? If I tried to cross the river, the ice would cut like glass, and the force of it would pull me under.

I followed it, like my father had done in the video—four

hundred more yards downstream. The air was full of mist
and fog; the landscape looked unrecognizable, much greener
than when my father had been here. I was about to retrace my
steps, thinking I had made a mistake, when I saw the house.

In the middle of the woods, two hundred yards from the
river's western edge, stood a simple wooden cabin. I stood still,
watching it to see if anyone was around. This house was the
mystery. It wasn't on any of the maps. There was no forest
ranger patrol hut marked with a red star here on any of the
visitor's website or guides; Cleo had driven this point home on
our flight. Nor was there an image of the house on the satellite
maps. There were no images of the boulders by the river, there
was nothing at all because this was the place that had been
blacked out.

This was the place my father had found the day before he
disappeared.

At first glance it looked exactly like a park ranger hut. I
found myself walking toward it. I summoned what courage
I had, thinking of how Cleo would behave in this situation. I
fought to feel secure knowing that the weapon she had given
me was safely strapped to my arm. I drew closer and saw the
telltale green National Park emblem; it was disguised to look
exactly like a ranger's hut. The door was ajar.

"Hello?" I called, peeking inside. It was only six by eight,
a simple wooden structure with a woodstove against the back
wall. Inside was a wooden picnic table and benches. A pile of
unused, folded blankets was stacked at the door, along with
what looked like an emergency supply of water. A cigarette
had been ground out on the concrete floor and the scent of
tobacco lingered.

"Hello?" I called out. I had the distinct feeling someone was watching me. Was someone here? I thought I could hear the sound of breathing. I spun around.

A Denali Park Ranger stood at the doorway of the house, cradling a rifle. He was about six feet tall and twenty-five, with reddish-brown hair and a ruddy face from the cold. He wore a forest-green uniform and hat, a metal badge pinned to his chest.

"You're trespassing," he said in a low, harsh voice. A second man stepped into the room from a doorway in the back I hadn't noticed. I lifted my arms overhead, so they would know I wasn't dangerous.

"I'm just . . . I'm lost," I told them. "I need help finding my way back to the camp."

The two men grabbed me by the shoulders, pushing me forward toward the back of the cabin. I felt the barrel of the gun at the back of my head.

"Please no," I whispered.

Was he going to shoot me against the wall? Is this what my father had stumbled across? Were these the men who killed him?

One of the men pulled open a door, which was concealed in the wooden boards, and pushed me into a dark closet. The door closed behind me.

The room was pitch-black.

Then I felt the floor sink beneath me.

A bright fluorescent light lit up the ceiling. The room I'd been forced into was in fact a steel box, some kind of elevator. The first ranger stood beside me, the gun still gripped in his hands. There had been no sign of this from outside.

"Where are we going?" I asked. I could feel the downward movement but I was overcome by claustrophobia. The guard didn't answer. He focused his eyes on the wall. How could this have not been visible from the outside? I hadn't noticed anything, no electricity cables, nothing, just the wilderness. All I wanted was the door to open. The stainless steel was polished and new, our reflections blurred against the steel.

The elevator stopped. All four doors slid open, revealing a brightly lit hallway made of cinder block.

"Follow me," he ordered.

How far was I from the surface? I should have concentrated harder. We had been in the elevator for what seemed like an endless amount of time, but we were moving slowly.

The guard led me into a long, brightly lit hallway. The walls were painted a yellowish white, like the hallways of a school. That wasn't the only part that reminded me of school—there was a specific smell, a mixture of hospital and cafeteria. Rows of long fluorescent lights lit the way along the hall. There were no windows, only closed doors five feet apart. Door after door after door: they all looked exactly alike, no numbers or any other distinguishing features.

I remember reading about the highest security prisons in the world, that they were underground. Is that what this was? A prison? Was this where Connor was? I was completely afraid of this place but at the same time I felt a spark of hope.

The guard opened one of the doors. Inside was a room with a sand-colored sofa, a black-and-white geometric rug, a painting of a ship at sea on the wall. My eyes were immediately drawn to a large window open halfway, with a view of a field with a red barn in the distance. I could feel summer air coming through it.

"Wait here," the guard said. "Someone will be here to see you soon."

The guard left the room. My jaw dropped; he left the door open. I was sure he would be keeping guard outside the hallway door, but when I went to look he wasn't in the hallway. No one was. The hallway of doors stretched as far as I could see. I looked at the ceiling, at the walls; surveillance cameras were mounted at every angle.

I was afraid to step over the threshold, back into the hallway. Nothing was stopping me, it was just a feeling that kept me from trying to escape right then. I sat down on the bed. I was surprised no one had asked me for my coat. I looked out the window at the pretty meadow. The blades of grass blew in the warm summer breeze; the air smelled of freshly cut grass and rain. Two cardinals sang from the branch of the tree.

The scene was so beguiling that I lost sense of time, or that I was alone, but mostly that what I was looking at was not real. We were not in western Massachusetts; there was no meadow outside this window. Yet the smell and the feel of the air, even the sound made it seem like it was completely real. For a minute or two, I watched, thinking it was real, too.

"Tanya." A woman's voice startled me.

"I'm Dr. Luanne Preston. It's so nice to finally meet you. We have heard so much about you." She smiled at me, a bright smile of perfectly straight teeth that looked very white against her plum-colored lipstick.

"What?" I heard myself say.

She was tall, with shoulder-length salt-and-pepper hair

turned under at her chin. She was pretty, too, in her fifties or early sixties. She wore a lab coat over a matching pale blue skirt set, clear stockings, black patent pumps, and a strand of pearls around her neck. "We know about you, Tanya. And now we'd like you to tell us what exactly you know about us."

"I . . . I don't know what you mean."

"Everything will be fine. You will be safe here with us, but you need to cooperate. Do you understand?" The doctor smiled after every sentence. She pulled up a chair and sat down in front of me. Another woman, a nurse, with curly short brown hair and a pale round face sat on a chair in the corner, transcribing.

I nodded. My palms were sweaty. I took a deep breath, trying to force myself to be calm. "I really don't know anything about this place," I said.

It was the truth. I had no idea from the maps that there would be an underground building or compound or whatever this place was.

"You just stumbled upon us?" She laughed at her own joke. She ran her finger along the string of pearls as she laughed.

"I was looking for . . . what happened to my father." I couldn't hide the anger in my voice as I spoke. "Was he killed here?" Tears welled in my eyes.

"We'll answer all your questions about your father soon enough. And on that front, you have nothing to fear."

"My father . . ." I didn't know what I felt. It was close to rage. These people had robbed me of my sole parent. They had put Beth and me through unspeakable suffering.

"Tell me who else knows we are here," the doctor persisted.

"What about Connor?" I stood up, but the guard

reappeared in the door. My knees buckled and my legs nearly gave out from under me.

She flashed an easy smile, almost as if she were a coach and I'd missed an easy shot. "We ask the questions, okay? Tell us the information we need."

I couldn't speak. I seethed with hatred. I hated her phony smile, her voice, and her cruel eyes. I would never tell her a thing.

"Tanya, let me explain," she continued. "This can be a very nice place to be. It can also be a not-so-nice place to be. Do you understand?"

"Yes," I forced out.

"I need the names of the two people who brought you here this morning."

"Harrison Worth," I snapped. "Alison, his secretary. They're the ones who brought me here. That's the truth." In a way, it was.

The woman stood up abruptly, pushing her chair behind her. Her smile disappeared. She glanced at the nurse and the guard, who both exited.

"That's enough for now. Maybe you're hungry, Tanya? Something tells me you'll remember more after lunch."

Chapter Eighteen

I followed behind the doctor past more doors and rooms that all looked exactly alike. We turned left, right, and then right again. I counted my footsteps for a reference of where we had come in from, starting at the elevator. I hated to not know where I was, but it was obvious this place was designed like a maze. Designed to disorient, and it was working.

I tried not to think of Cleo and Gretchen. They *were* professionals at this sort of thing, I kept telling myself, whatever this sort of thing even was. I'd seen how they'd behaved; they clearly knew how to get in and out of dangerous places undetected. They must have fled in the smoke and confusion, as I had. If they'd been hurt, they would have screamed, cried for help. I'd been the only one screaming. No, they'd slipped away and were probably getting their hands on a new plane. Cleo was the kind of person who always had a backup plan. That's what I told myself to stay strong, anyway.

We reached an elevator, and she swiped a card. The steel

door opened. It was two feet by two feet. I stood between the doctor and the guard. The elevator didn't feel as though it moved at all, even though we were in there for over a minute.

The doors on all sides slid upward, and I found myself standing in a round room. I blinked for a moment, not trusting my eyes. It was an opulent dining hall. Oak tables set with fresh flowers, a candle at each centerpiece. Chandeliers hung from the ceiling casting a pretty, soft glow. The "windows" looked out to a meadow and lane.

"You might want to sit over there."

Dr. Preston pointed to a table in the corner where a man sat alone eating a sandwich. My legs nearly gave out from under me.

My father is here. My father . . .

He was a little thinner, his hair a little greyer. But that slender face, those gentle eyes behind the wire-rim frames were the same.

He's alive. My father is alive.

He wore jeans and a T-shirt, the kind of thing he'd wear on a Saturday afternoon back in Amherst, relaxing around the shed. It was summer there. What was it here? This was the place that time forgot. Seasons didn't matter. Nothing did—not even death, apparently.

I wanted to run to him, to call his name. I stood, unable to move.

I looked around for the doctor, but she was gone. Only then did my feet move toward the table. He was facing a window, so he didn't see me. I looked at his breakfast, scrambled eggs and wheat toast, coffee and juice. All so normal. Even Tabasco sauce, which he loved.

"Dad," I breathed.

He didn't turn. Had he heard me? I reached out to touch his shoulder. My hand was visibly trembling. "Dad?"

He turned at the touch and his eyes met mine. They flickered behind his glasses. A smile appeared briefly. "It's me, Dad. It's Tanya." Everything else I wanted to say died in my throat. A painful lump lodged itself there. Tears blurred my vision. Was he going to stand up? Hug me? Wrap his arms around me and hold me tightly? He sat there staring at me as though I were someone he knew but couldn't quite place.

"Tanya?" he finally whispered.

He reached forward, covering my hand in his. I noticed his skin looked pale and his hands shook, too.

"Sit down. Have breakfast with me. Or how about lunch?"

I did as he said, but I felt as if I were watching myself from a distance. My limbs obeyed commands that were too surreal to process. I wondered if *I* had died. My dad turned, beckoning a waiter, who carried over a tray of food. On the tray was a beautiful green salad, a steaming bowl of penne with tomato sauce and grated cheese, a glass of sparkling water with lemon. I poked at the fresh greens. They looked as if they'd been plucked that morning. My father must have read my mind.

"They grow it here," he said. "There's a greenhouse on-site."

The food did look delicious. I knew I wouldn't be able to touch it. I felt an anguish too unbearable to name. My father was alive, but this man across from me was not the Michael Barrett who'd left for Cambodia all those months ago.

"Dad," I whispered. "We thought you were dead. Beth still thinks you're dead."

"I'm not dead," he said in a quiet monotone.

"You've been here all this time?"

He nodded.

"But you didn't tell us. You couldn't, I'm guessing." *Hoping. Praying.*

Again with the noncommittal nod.

"We thought you were dead," I repeated, enunciating the words carefully. My voice rose in frustration. "Do you understand that? Do you know what you put us through? Do you even miss us? Miss Beth? Miss me?"

He nodded once more, blinking several times. "I do. I do, very much."

Maybe it was time to try a different tack. "Dad, Harrison tried to kill me."

My father turned his vacant, rheumy eyes in my direction. "Harrison is my best friend. He's your godfather. He would never hurt you."

It was obvious he wasn't going to tell me anything I needed to know. Either he knew he was being watched, or he had been brainwashed. Given that he was more interested in his meal than seeing his daughter, the latter seemed more likely. I wasn't sure which was worse.

"Is Connor here?" I asked. My voice caught on his name.

Again, he didn't answer. He took a bite of his eggs. "We are doing such amazing things here. Things that are going to change the world—"

"Dad," I interrupted.

"Listen to me, Tanya. Imagine a place where no living creature ever gets lost again. Remember how sad you were when Bootsy disappeared? How you searched for her in the woods every day after school?" His voice had a soft lilt.

There were people all around, but no one seemed to be paying attention to us. I glanced at the ceiling, at the walls, searching for tiny microphones or cameras.

"No one will be lost in the future," he added. "I have so much time to work here, and the work is so close to being finished. Nothing to worry about." His eyes were drier now, but still glassy, like his smile. "Do you know what else?"

I shook my head. I felt sick and empty. I could see now what Dr. Luanne Preston meant: this could be a not-very-nice place.

"There's an ocean here," he finished.

I raised my eyebrows. "An ocean?"

He laughed again, more like a chuckle. Not his real laugh. Not the laugh my real dad had. His eyes darted across the room. The doctor was walking toward us. For the second time, my father reached out for my hand. He spoke quickly. "The air and water come from outside." He dropped my hand and took a bite of toast. It was the first time his voice had sounded normal, the first time he'd appeared even remotely like himself.

"Tanya." The doctor stood over us. She placed a small cupful of pink and white pills in front of my father. He took the pills and swallowed them.

"Michael," she said. "Did you have a nice visit with your daughter?"

I watched my dad nod with polite and enthusiastic subservience, like a child. They'd destroyed him. This sick woman or someone just like her had killed the Michael Barrett who'd been my father. *Dr. Luanne Preston*. What kind of a doctor was she? I wished I'd grabbed the pills she'd given my dad and thrown them at her. It was only the desperate hope of finding Connor that kept me in line. I had to behave right now.

"Michael, it's time to go back to the office," Dr. Preston said.

"Yes, I suppose it is." He stood.

She turned to me. "His program is really coming along. Your father is doing a wonderful job here. Our hope is that you can work for us, too, someday."

Our hope. It wasn't hard to smile at that. Masking the horror took some effort.

"Goodbye Tanya," my father said formally. He held out his hand for me to shake. I could feel the watchful eyes of Dr. Luanne Preston on me as I shook back.

"Bye." I bit my bottom lip in an attempt to fight back tears.

I had to ask to see the beach. There was something my father was trying to tell me. Something I didn't understand yet. I watched my father make his way out of the dining hall. The disassociated feeling—of being trapped in a bad dream—began to fade. The anger returned.

"When will I see him again?" I demanded.

"When you answer our questions," Dr. Preston replied.

"I already told you everything I know."

"Tanya, if you cooperate, you can have a nice life here, like your father does. You can work beside him, like you would have done at MapOut." The elevator descended from some hidden place in the ceiling. "How about a tour?" she asked pleasantly, heading toward it. She swiped her key card and one of the doors opened.

Inside, the elevator looked more like a security checkpoint. A black-uniformed security guard sat at a desk, a submachine gun on the table in front of him, next to an office phone. Two screens lit up behind him black and white, hazy with static. She picked up the phone—connected by a cord to the receiver—and pressed the buttons quickly.

A voice answered. "Dr. Preston 4476. Outgoing call."

A sound rang out, like a dial tone.

A man's voice anwered. I recognized it immediately. It was Harrison.

One of the screens flickered, and the interference faded. A crystal clear image of Harrison appeared. He was dressed business-casual, sitting at his vast desk in his plush Amherst MapOut office. Judging from the angle, the camera was hidden somewhere in the ceiling. I shuddered involuntarily. Dr. Preston had probably watched me from this angle when I'd greeted Harrison in that office on my first day. Maybe my dad had, too. Harrison was so far away, and yet he still filled me with fear. Or maybe it was the fear of knowing I would always be watched no matter where I was, from this point forward.

The second screen flickered, and I appeared in sharp black and white, in real time. I glanced around in a panic, struggling to determine where the camera was. I couldn't.

"Harrison," Dr. Preston said. "Tanya is here. I've explained that she can help us here. Work for our company."

Harrison's face was damp and pale. Dark circles ringed his eyes. He looked terrible. "So our deal stands," he choked out. "Connor will be released."

"Yes, our deal stands," Dr. Preston said, sounding bored.

"Though I have to add that it should have been much easier to negotiate. I hope you'll reflect on that."

Before he could respond, she pressed a button on the phone. The screens went black. Only now did I realize that the security guard had been staring at me the entire time, unblinking. I wondered what he would do if I suddenly lunged at Dr. Preston. If I pulled out the weapon Cleo had given me from beneath my sleeve and shot her. I still wasn't sure exactly what it did. Would it kill her? Knock her out? Actually, it wasn't that hard to guess what the guard would do. He'd pump me full of submachine-gun bullets, and then this elevator would take my body somewhere to be erased from existence.

Dr. Preston punched a code into the keypad, and the door slid open. I followed her into another small chamber— more of a real elevator, a steel box. When the door closed behind us, I heard the hum of machinery. I couldn't tell if we were moving up or down. I told myself to stay calm. But it was impossible. Creeping terror took hold. My breathing became labored. *They don't even need to kill me,* I realized. *I've already been erased from existence.* Cleo and Gretchen were the only two people who knew I was here. If they were dead—and there was only so much denial I could indulge— then I'd have to figure out a way to escape. Most likely I would die trying.

"Tanya, are you all right?" Dr. Preston asked.

I glared at her. The door opened onto a nondescript hall.

"Try to relax," she said, her voice businesslike. "You aren't in any danger." She led me up a stairwell to an adjoining identical hallway. I furiously concentrated on my inner compass. I was pretty certain this hall faced north . . . no, northeast. But because it was impossible to tell if we had gone up or down in the elevators, I was disoriented.

We came to a door, and I glanced wildly up, down, and sideways, hoping to feel that invisible tug. I didn't, but for the first time I spotted tiny black orbs in the lighting fixtures: surveillance cameras.

Dr. Preston swiped her card through the door handle. My lips parted slightly. I wasn't sure why I was surprised; maybe I'd been expecting to be escorted to an interrogation cell. This was more like a living room spread from some glitzy real-estate website. White sofas ringed a pale blue rug; huge windows looked out to the sea.

"This could be where you live," said Dr. Preston. "Isn't it spectacular?"

My body went cold. I shivered again, wrapping the heavy lead jacket around me, tucking my hands into the sleeves.

"I'll show you where you'll work alongside your father," she added.

She moved to another door inside the house. It was made of gorgeous pine, and it didn't require a swipe card—there was just a regular brass knob. *Just like a real home.* She turned it, revealing a high-tech office. It was as large as the renovated third floor at MapOut, only there were no cubicles. The desks were all empty, except for one. My father occupied it, sitting in front of two monitors, his back to me. The air was filled with a strange sound, pumped seemingly from every direction: a drumbeat, then a whoosh like a wave, then another drumbeat. On the screen was a shaky black-and-white image, moving in time with the rhythm.

"What is that?" I asked Dr. Preston.

Similar images played from the hundreds of high-definition monitors around the room. The sound was so familiar, yet I couldn't place it.

"Why don't you ask your father?" she encouraged gently. "Go on. He's waiting."

I walked over to him, my legs shaky. I almost hesitated when I reached for his shoulder. It was a reflex from home; he hated being disturbed when he worked. He looked up and smiled before I could make contact.

"Tanya, sit down. I'm anxious to show you what we're making here."

I slumped down in the empty chair behind him. Only when I exhaled did I notice I'd been holding my breath.

"This is a heart," he said. "Did you know that everyone has a unique heartbeat? Think of it as an aural fingerprint. A signature in sound. The heart is always sending a message to the world."

I couldn't follow him. The shock still hadn't worn off. "I . . . don't know what you mean, Dad," I stammered.

"What I mean is, unlike fingerprints, the heart can always be heard. We are finding a way to track everyone by his or her heartbeat, starting at birth. In a way, we'll be mapping humanity itself."

His tone was genial, robotic. He sounded like a tele-marketer. Reaching forward, he switched the image on the monitor; it flashed to an aerial view of the room we were in now. We seemed to be sitting closer together than I'd realized. He typed in the words: heartbeat detection Michael Barrett. The computer flashed an image of my father in real time facing the screen. He typed in the word: track Michael Barrett.

"We won't need surveillance cameras anymore," he said. "Just satellites in the sky. This is what I mean, Tanya. No living creature will ever be lost again."

In the reflection of the computer screen I saw Dr. Preston standing behind us.

"Did you show Tanya the beach?" he asked. "The water and fresh air are so nice."

"Not yet," replied Dr. Preston coldly. "We have some business to attend to first. Come with me, Tanya."

"Bye, sweetheart," my dad said in the same distant voice. His fingers were already typing again; the monitor flashed to a satellite image of the Earth.

I couldn't say goodbye.

"Would you like to see the beach?" Dr. Preston asked.

At this point, if she'd pointed a gun at my head and asked if I wanted to die, I would have agreed. I would have agreed to anything. Maybe this was how they'd turned my father into this zombie. Not through pills, but through the certain knowledge that he would never be leaving, ever. He *was* dead.

"Why not?" I said.

She led me back into the house, then downstairs to another nondescript hallway. This one wasn't silent, however. The sounds of seagulls and waves grew louder with each step we took toward the door at the hall's end. *"Mapmakers don't like dead-ends,"* my father had been fond of saying; now dead ends were his only option. Again she swiped the key card; again the door slid open. We stepped onto a concrete floor with concrete walls. A second set of doors slid open and I winced at a blast of sunshine.

A moment later, I stepped onto pale, fine sand. Clear blue water slopped down into a large pool, and soft waves rolled in. I felt sick. There were children here. Two boys, maybe nine or ten—they must have been twins—batted around a beach ball. A girl of about six played with a toy mermaid at the edge of the water. The walls looked like a real sky, with moving clouds, a hot sun. A teenage lifeguard was perched in a chair, complete with sunblock on his nose. I guessed if you were a child you would think this was real. Maybe for the children it was better than real. Maybe they'd never known anything else. In that way, it *was* real. This was my dad's real life now, too. And mine.

The girl playing with her mermaid doll glanced up at me. I could see a red scar on her chest, right over her bathing suit. The boys had the scar, too, in the same spot: slightly to the left. So did the lifeguard. My father's words reverberated in my mind: *"No living creature will ever be lost again."* And all the heartbeats in that room. A sickening thought formed. Like my father, these people were all being tracked. He probably had the same scar, too.

I scanned the walls, the water. My father had mentioned the water, the air, that it came from outside. Somewhere behind these walls there must be air shafts and huge water pipes. Which meant there might be a way out.

"Take off your shoes," Dr. Preston encouraged. "Make yourself at home."

I did as she said. The sand was real, hot from the fake sun. I dipped my feet in the water as it softly lapped toward the shore. Only then did I catch a faint whiff of chlorine mixed with the smell of salt water.

"Isn't it wonderful?" Dr. Preston said.

I tried to hide any emotion. "It feels real."

"It feels *better*," she said. "There's no danger here. No sharks or undertow. The children can play freely. If they start to struggle, they would not drown. If you live here and work for us, you can use this beach whenever you want." She took a deep breath and her tone shifted. "Now let me show you where you'll live if you don't cooperate."

After pulling my shoes and socks back on, I followed her into the cold concrete antechamber. The door closed behind us, and the fluorescent overhead lights popped on. Once again, I heard that faint hum. Again, I couldn't tell if we'd moved. But we must have moved, because when the door opened again, it wasn't to the same hall through which we'd entered.

There was a rancid smell in the air. The lights were different here: blue and dim. A machine-gun-wielding guard, dressed in the same plain black uniform as the guard I'd seen before, wandered up and down the narrow corridor. It was lined with metal doors that stretched for at least a hundred yards.

Then I heard a muted scream.

This was a prison. Dr. Preston nudged me forward. We passed the guard, who seemed to study my face intently. I peeked through the tiny windows of each cell as we passed, expecting to see some kind of torture scene, but the cells were all empty, devoid even of furniture.

Dr. Preston stopped outside one, seemingly at random.

Through the thick bulletproof glass I could see a bare mattress, someone hunched over in pain. Dr. Preston rapped on the window. The person started, whirling to stare at us with wide eyes. His face was bruised, swollen. At first I didn't recognize him.

"Connor?" My voice wavered unsurely.

The door swung open. He looked at me but didn't speak. He didn't move from his place on the floor. His eyes were filled with fear.

He looked broken. I wanted to reach out to him. I turned to Dr. Preston. "What have you done to him?"

"He was uncooperative. We're hoping he'll change his mind."

"Can I talk to him?"

She waved the guard over. "Of course. That's why I brought you here." Then she smiled down at Connor. "Young man? You have a visitor."

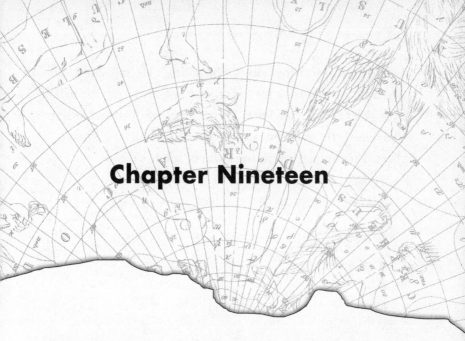

Chapter Nineteen

I didn't hear the door close behind me or the electronic click of the lock. Connor sat on a mattress, gaping up at me like a frightened child. He'd been so badly beaten. I wondered if his cheekbones or nose were broken. His left arm was in a cast. I stepped toward him. Before I knew it, he was sweeping me into his arms.

I hugged him as tightly as I could. His skin felt hot, but he was shivering. He rested his head on mine and I could feel his body shake with silent sobs. As much as it pained me, I hadn't realized how much I craved human contact until this moment. This place was inhuman.

"What did they do to you?" I murmured.

"Look up," he whispered as we held each other. Slowly I lifted my eyes.

Surveillance cameras were mounted in all four corners of the cell. Of course they were. Could they hear us, too?

Even if we stood this close whispering? He withdrew from my embrace and took my wrist, opening my hand. We locked eyes. I knew exactly what he meant to do. In that instant, we were little children again. With his shaky forefinger, he started tracing letters in the palm of my hand.

E
S
C
A
P
E

I took his hand and returned his fearful gaze, mimicking what he'd done. There was only one option and I knew it was time. I would risk my life now. If I failed, I would die and I would be forgotten, erased. If I succeeded, if by some miracle I managed to get us out of here, I would tell the world about this awful place. I traced out the letters:

G
U
N

I touched my forearm, felt the slim strip of the weapon Cleo had given me. I slipped the cylinder from inside my sleeve to my wrist. His eyes flashed to it and then back to mine again. I knew he understood. It was hidden from the guards and Dr. Preston, concealed by my jacket sleeve. I felt for the screen on the side, touching my thumb to it once.

What would it do exactly? I wished I'd asked Cleo to explain it better to me. Laser meant nothing. All I could think of was *Star Wars*.

The door slid open.

"It's time to say goodbye to Connor," Dr. Preston announced. She stepped into the cell. The guard stood behind her in the hallway.

"I can't!" I cried. I swept him into a tight hug. "You take the doctor," I whispered in his ear. "I'll get the guard."

"Enough, get ahold of yourself." She whirled to the guard. "Separate them," she ordered.

The guard strode into the cell. Gripping the weapon, I whirled and aimed, pressing my thumb to the screen again. Nothing. Nothing emanated from the end, neither light nor sound. He lunged at me, pushing me roughly to the door. Why wasn't it working? I pointed it at him again, holding my thumb down, aiming at his right eye.

All of a sudden he froze, solid. It was as if he'd transformed into a statue. His right eye turned black. The pupil and iris disappeared. For a second I thought I might vomit. He fell backward against the cinder block wall and tumbled to the floor.

Without hesitating, Connor took the key card from the guard and the gun from his holster. Dr. Preston dashed into the hallway.

"Help!" she barked.

I chased after her. The moment she turned back to me, I pointed the laser at her left eye and pressed the button. Her body stiffened in the same way, her pupil dilating like a spreading stain of black ink. This time I didn't feel the slightest bit queasy. I watched as she hit the floor, her head smashing against the concrete. I felt nothing.

I grabbed Connor, pulling him down the hall. He shoved the key card in my hand. Maybe he was worried that he was too shaky. But I was no better. I swiped the key card; the prison doors slid open. We were in a corridor I didn't recognize, also lined with doors. I tried one. It didn't open. Neither did the second or third. I was frantic, desperate for a place to hide, when I realized all the doors were phony. Like so much of this place, they were part of an elaborate mirage.

Sirens blared.

Connor looked at me, eyes wide.

"My dad said the air and water come from outside," I said, searching for any possible escape. "He was trying to tell me something. There must be a way out through the vents or water tunnels."

"They would be inside the walls," he whispered.

At the end of the hall, a door opened. Two guards ran out. Again, Connor didn't hesitate. He fired. Bullets ricocheted off the walls, nearly deafening me. My ears stung and rang. But he succeeded in scaring them off. Crouching low, the guards quickly ducked through another door to the side. The moment their escape route closed, Connor ran past it and through the door from which they'd entered. I was fast on his heels. The doors shut and we were back on one of the elevators.

I swiped my key card, and the light overhead turned on, along with the hum. Maybe twenty seconds later, it opened on the widest hall I'd encountered yet, with a marble floor. It was lined with carved wooden doors, beautiful and elegant, like I'd seen inside the "house." My ringing ears perked up; I could hear the crash of waves. We were near the beach. I worked on one side of the hall, pulling open every door, identical lush room after identical lush room—until I opened up on a room with a view of the ocean. There was nowhere to hide. None of the doors had locks. It looked as though you could open the window and run on the beach for miles.

I felt the "window" where the air was coming through, the large thin screen displaying 3-D images of a virtual outside world. I knew it must be connected to an electrical source behind the wall.

Without a word, Connor nodded. Together we tore it down, using the butt of the machine gun to smash the bolts. As it collapsed to the floor, it revealed a narrow space full of electrical wires, vents, and pipes.

We climbed inside. There was only one right direction to go: up.

The only option was to the left or right. I chose left, as it would take us back toward the elevator. The elevators went up; that I knew for certain. We hit another intersection; I chose left again. As quietly as I could, I scrambled through the mass of wires, Connor at my feet, farther and farther from the hole in the wall.

All around us were muffled voices and sirens. The narrow duct grew darker. My head struck a wall. We'd come to a dead end. In the pitch-darkness we were trapped at the end of a tunnel.

But I felt a breeze overhead. I felt with my fingers and they brushed over a metal grate. "I think there's something above us." It was embedded in the surrounding concrete. I punched it but it didn't budge. I punched it again and again until my hand was bleeding. I looked down into the darkness. The alarms sounded from within echoing inside the walls of the underground compound.

"Give me the laser," Connor said. "Your weapon."

It took some maneuvering in the cramped space even to hand it to him. I was sweating now. Connor aimed the laser gun at the edges where the metal was sealed to the concrete. A brilliant spot of white light began to sizzle right overhead, followed by a cascade of dust and rubble. I coughed and held my breath, then tugged. It was loose, but not enough. He aimed again and again, until it finally fell on top of my head.

I didn't even feel the pain. My eyes were greeted by the sweetest sight I'd ever seen: a sixty-three-foot ladder, ending in another grate. And beyond that grate was grey sky. Real sky. I shoved the grate against the dead end.

This must have been where the fresh air was being pumped in through the ventilation system. The sound of machinery hummed from outside. I could smell the cold, feel it against my skin. Wild hope coursed through my exhausted body. I started up the ladder. Connor was right behind me.

Blood from the gash in my forehead dripped into my eyes. I could feel the sting, but it distracted me from the numbness of my fingers as we clawed our way toward those Arctic clouds. Just seven more feet . . .

"Are you okay?" Connor whispered below me.

"Hand me the laser."

Once again, I burned away the grate bolts. I didn't look down; I didn't want to have a flash of vertigo and take

Connor down with me. The moment the grate was loose, I shoved it out of the way and clambered out into the frozen wilderness. I gave Connor a hand as I scanned the area, panting, my breath coming in icy bursts. An uneven pile of boulders surrounded us on three sides. There was no person in sight; the house was nowhere to be seen, and the only distinguishable sound was the river. The air smelled of damp earth and sweet flowers.

"Can you run?" I gasped at him.

I must have looked as awful as he did because he replied, "Can you?"

"Of course." I stepped out from behind the boulders—clearly they'd been placed to hide the grate—and spotted the river, the mountains in the background. Between us and the river was a slope of green-and-brown tundra, a patch of pink flowers growing alongside the riverbank. In a flash, I knew exactly where I was and where I needed to go.

Removed from that disorienting prison, I had my gift back. And for the first time in my life, it truly felt like a gift.

"There's a road one mile four hundred and sixty-five yards from that bend right there. A straight line through the woods, and we'll hit it. It's where the tourist bus goes back to Camp Denali. They run every few hours—"

"Stay still." I felt Connor gently wipe the blood on the side of my face away with his shirtsleeve.

"You go," I said. "I can't leave my dad."

Connor blinked at me, his bruised face twisted in a grimace. "No way. Forget it. I'm not letting you go back inside. You'll never get out again. You won't be able to get your dad out. I'm sorry." He pulled me close to him. "I know you'll be able to map that place now, but it's still too dangerous. We'll get help. We'll get your dad out, I promise."

He took my hands in his, his eyes filled with fear. "We have to run now. We have to leave here or they will find us and kill us."

I nodded. I felt a familiar pain in my chest. He was right. I had to leave my dad behind now. I had to cling to the hope that we'd come back and rescue him, or that he'd manage his own escape when the time was right. I would cling in the same way I'd clung to the hope that Cleo and Gretchen had escaped with their lives—that they were too wily and too fast on their feet to be incinerated in that explosion. They were at large, like us. And they knew a piece of the truth, too.

In silence, Connor and I bolted across the field to the river. *Don't look back,* I told myself, *just keep running.* We ran so fast I could barely breathe. Still, I felt the tears streaming down my face.

Nobody chased after us. Only after the panic subsided, after I'd stopped holding my breath and waiting for a burst of machine-gun fire—only after we'd waded across the frozen river and were limping through the woods—only then did I start wondering why.

And the simple reason occurred to me: they couldn't.

They would never risk giving themselves or their location away. And there was no need to. Would the authorities believe two battered kids, one who was a fugitive from the law, the other who was supposed to be at college, that there was a secret compound in the middle of Denali National Park? It couldn't be found. It *wouldn't* be found, not ever.

Which meant we really would have to figure out a way to get back in.

By the time we reached the deserted road, the sun was beginning to edge to the west. It would barely set this far north, just skirt below the horizon. We sat in the dirt, holding each other. There was nothing left to say. Or maybe we were too tired to say it. Before long, a dark green bus appeared. We waved to it frantically, and it screeched to a stop. The doors opened. "What happened to you?" the bus driver asked. He was a large man with a friendly smile.

"We fell in the river," I said. "It was stupid. Sorry."

"Get in," he said. "We'll get you checked out back at the camp."

I could feel all eyes on us as we crept on board and settled into a seat, shivering. A woman behind me tapped me on the back.

"Would you like this?" She held out an army green blanket.

"Thank you," I said, between chattering teeth. I wrapped the blanket around both of us. Outside the bus window, a flock of geese crossed the sky. The clouds broke a little; where the sun had just been a fuzzy spot of yellow, it poked through with intensity. The wilderness stretched out untouched on either side of us. I felt Connor's hand in mine.

When we were alone, I would tell him about everything that had happened, Connor would tell me everything that had happened to him. There was one thing I knew: to be safe we had to stay in public spaces. We had to be near people, we could not be alone. Not now, not ever. Not until we held his father accountable.

• • •

At the Camp Denali Hotel Lodge, Connor and I sat on one of the sofas surrounding the large fireplace, waiting for someone to arrive from the infirmary. Even as my clothes began to dry, I felt a coldness in my bones that I thought would never leave me. I watched the flames flicker and burn. I thought of the lies we'd have to tell the nurse or doctor, about the names we'd have to make up. We couldn't use our real identities anymore. If we were to survive, we were going to have to start from scratch.

"Was your dad the one who brought you to that place?" I whispered.

Connor shook his head. "No."

"You're saying Harrison wasn't involved?"

"This is Rytech, Tanya. His investors. Your dad was so much more brilliant than any of us realized. And by the time my dad figured it out, it was too late." He opened his mouth as if to add something, then bit his lip, afraid of what he was about to say. "It was you, too, Tanya. He was using my life as a bargaining chip. Telling them to keep me alive in exchange for you. My dad convinced them that you have a 'gift.'

That's what they call it, the way you map things in your head, your sense of direction. They want to run tests on you, to see if there's anything to his claim. And then most likely exploit you, like they have your dad."

Connor looked into his hands as though searching for the right words. "Tanya, I just want you to know . . . I'm not my father. I'm not like him at all."

"I know you're not."

"But I have to tell you something. They did something to me in there."

I turned to him. Trembling, he pulled his hand from mine. Slowly, with shaking fingers, he unbuttoned the top few buttons of his shirt. A giant scar covered the left side of his chest, like a slash mark.

"They have my heartbeat."

At first I couldn't understand what he was trying to tell me. Then I recalled the monitors, my father's new mantra, *"No living creature will ever be lost again."*

"They put their tracking device inside me. It follows everyone by their heartbeat. It's not safe for me to be here with you. I'm putting you in danger."

I looked at the people in the hotel, trying to distinguish their faces. Men and woman of all ages, children and teenagers, all mingling happily, drinking hot cider by the fire, warming themselves. Who among them was watching us? Who was following us?

"Not necessarily," I said, taking off the jacket Cleo had given to me, the jacket that hid body heat from radar surveillance. It was still cold and wet from the river. "Put it on. They can't track you through this." I wasn't sure that was true, but if it convinced him to stay put, it was worth the lie. "Cleo gave it to me and it saved my life."

He returned my gaze. He knew what I was thinking. They would kill him once they tracked him down, they would silence his heartbeat forever. They would take him off the map. Once again, I glanced around the lobby: at the old couple sitting near us at the fireplace, at the family of four eating dinner in the restaurant, at a single woman sitting alone at the bar.

"They're probably trying to locate us now," Connor whispered.

I looked into his eyes, the flames from the fire reflected in them.

"They may be," I whispered back. "But if it's inside of you where can we hide?"

Connor looked at me, trying his best to be strong. "They can catch me, but we can't let them get you. You have to go."

I felt my hands shake. I knew he was right. I looked around the cabin lobby. It was such a happy, warm, cozy place but to me it felt like a ticking bomb. My eyes moved to the doorways, to the exit sign. Who was coming in? A family with two young children? But who was behind them, they could already be here, watching us.

"I know a place we can go."

Connor looked up at me. He looked pale, his skin whitish grey. He was clearly sick, ill from his time in the underground cell.

"Where?" he whispered.

"Cleo's house. It's completely off the grid. There is nothing that could track the monitor they put inside you there. We'll be safe for a while at least."

Cleo would take care of us, I thought. If she was alive. She had to be, I told myself. *Please God, make Cleo be alive.*

From the cabin windows I could see in the distance the park bus coming down the single road. The bus would take us outside the park. After that I wasn't sure how exactly we would get to Cleo's but at least we would try.

"Connor." I reached out my hand to him. His skin felt icy cold. "The bus is coming, it's our chance."

"Go without me."

"No."

He looked away from me.

An announcement sounded through the hotel lobby: "The last visitor transportation shuttle will be leaving at eight thirty P.M., in front of the North Face Lodge."

I felt my breath go short with panic. We had to leave; we couldn't stay, but I knew I wouldn't leave without him.

"Please, Connor." Outside the sky was pink and grey. "Please come with me. I need your help. I can't leave you here."

He stood and shook his head.

"You have to go alone." He nodded toward the families with duffel bags and young children heading to the door. "Get on the bus with them, and no one will find you."

I felt the sting of tears. I had already abandoned my father. I had lost Cleo and Gretchen. There was no way I was losing him, too. His eyes shifted nervously around the room, as though he expected someone from RyTech to walk in the door at any moment.

I took his hand and his eyes met mine. I wrote in his palm.

T

R

U

S

T

M

E

Connor stared back at me. "Okay," he said finally.

The bus was already idling, packed and warm. We were

the last ones on. I wondered if anyone would notice that we were the only people carrying nothing at all. The seats and overhead racks were full of camping gear, knapsacks, and sleeping bags. We slid into an empty row at the back.

I held my breath until we pulled away.

We moved slowly, bumping along the narrow dirt road. The remnants of sunlight were fading, the sky turning charcoal.

Would they be waiting for us at the edge of the National Park when the bus left us near the highway? Or were they already on the bus, following us?

I pressed my forehead against the cool glass window. I felt myself rising up, looking down at the park from the night sky. The six million acres of land hidden in darkness: the animals, the mountains, the lakes, and the people. Everything hidden, except the headlights of our bus, moving along the road.

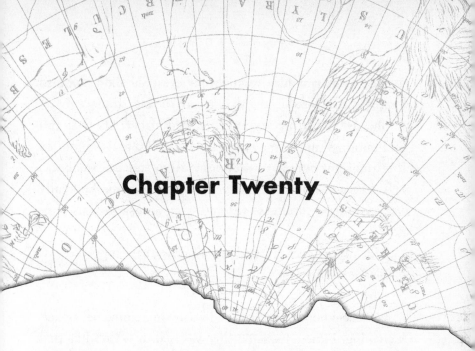

Chapter Twenty

When the bus stopped for the first time and its doors hissed open, I tried to squint past the frosty glare of the parking lot. I tried to make sense of the shadowy wilderness beyond it. That wilderness might be our only safe haven. The driver plodded down the stairs. He was pale, middle-aged, and heavyset. He looked bored with his job. That was good. Maybe he wouldn't notice us.

Connor lay still beside me. His breathing was loud and heavy, his damp hair matted to his forehead. He was sick from what they'd sewn inside his chest. For all I knew, the procedure Rytech had performed might kill him before the device could even alert our pursuers to our exact location within the millimeter.

I turned back to the window, watching as the driver unloaded camping gear from the carrier below, as the tourists made their way to their cars. Happy people going home, going back to their lives . . .

One woman suddenly caught my eyes. She didn't look so happy. She lingered in the shadows of the bus stop.

She seemed to be waiting. I stared at her. She was tall and bundled up in an oversized parka, baseball cap pulled low and tight over her head, ponytail jutting out the back. Her face was obscured, but her visor moved methodically back and forth, hidden eyes sweeping across the bus windows.

When those eyes reached my window, they stopped.

I jerked in my seat.

Cleo.

Her cheekbones. Her lips . . . I wasn't imagining her or hallucinating. I knew I wasn't; this was real. It wasn't like that wintry day back in Amherst when I'd forgotten my father had died and thought I saw his footsteps in the snow. To be fair, those footsteps were real, but my father hadn't left them. Connor's father had.

As a car pulled out of the lot, the sweeping flash of its headlights illuminated the woman's face. It *was* Cleo.

She returned my pregnant stare. Then she whirled and vanished into the shadows. Before I could move, the driver had closed the doors.

"Our next and final stop is Denali Viewpoint North," the driver announced. His voice was gravelly over the loudspeaker. "Twenty minutes."

With a puff of exhaust, we pulled back onto the only road in and out of Denali National Park. My hands cupped around my face against the cold glass, I peered outside. The bus stop was deserted. Excitement leapt inside me. Only Cleo would be so adept at concealing herself. If it were someone else—someone random; someone tall, strong, and agile—I would have spotted her again, trying to hide.

But I saw nothing. Cleo was too professional for that.

She's alive. She survived. She wanted to make sure I know.

I rested my head on Connor's shoulder, closing my eyes just for a second, or so I told myself. But at some point I must have fallen asleep, because the next thing I remembered was being woken by the jolt of the bus coming to another stop.

"This is the final Denali National Park destination," the driver said over the loudspeaker. "Everybody off."

I sat up and blinked, rubbing my eyes. We were at the outer edge of another parking lot. There were fewer cars here, and the blacktop was dimmer.

"Connor," I whispered, pushing him gently to wake him. His skin was still pale. I touched my hand to his forehead; it was burning hot.

"You have a fever," I said. Instinctively I reached for a water bottle, but then realized I had nothing with me. No water, no money, no car, no phone, no way out of here.

Connor groaned. He was conscious, at least. I helped him out the door, and we headed out to a stretch of mowed grass near the parking lot entrance. My first thought was to beg for a ride from one of the people from the bus, but we only made it about twenty feet before Connor fell to his knees and collapsed.

The bus emitted a cloud of exhaust as the driver closed the door and turned around, heading back.

Under the moonlight, Connor looked even paler than before, the veins beneath his eyes visible through the skin.

Panic seeped in. My eyes remained on Connor as the parking lot emptied . . . car after car pulling out, filled with the passengers from our bus. I straightened and whirled around; there was no sign of Cleo. I shivered in the cold. Had I imagined her? When the last SUV roared into the night, I found myself sprinting toward it and crying out. But whoever was inside, snug and safe with the windows up, didn't hear me.

We were alone.

Under the night sky, with the tundra stretching out for miles in every direction, I saw for the very first time how small and how helpless Connor and I were. The lone highway was the only escape. Even if Rytech was tracking us, we could easily die from exposure, from hypothermia, from an animal attack. We *would* die. Maybe that had been Rytech's plan all along.

I tried my hardest to be strong. I tried to not to cry; I tried to hide my anxiety. I put my arm around Connor, murmuring that we would be okay. He was sweating and shivering at the same time.

I thought of all the terrible truths I'd confronted today. Seeing my father so changed, brainwashed. Leaving him, when my goal was to rescue him. Would he ever make it out? Would I ever see him again? Would he ever be the same? At least I knew he was alive. But what about Cleo? *Had* I hallucinated her? What about Gretchen?

I brushed the tears away. As hopeless as I felt, the here-and-now was that Connor's life depended on me. We couldn't just stay here uncovered for the night. The temperature was dropping. I got up and scoured the area for shelter. But there was only low growth trees and brush and the empty parking lot with the dim fluorescent lights.

I would have to make my way to the edge of the highway. Find someone to call 911 for help. Before someone from Rytech got to us.

"We just have to walk to the highway," I breathed to Connor, my voice shaking. It was a third of a mile away—maybe 600 yards. "We have to get a ride to the nearest hospital."

Connor's hand in mine was sickly, warm, and damp. He made it a few steps in the direction of the highway, then stumbled and fell again.

In the silence, as I lifted him to his feet, I thought I heard the sound of a car coming. Not from the highway—but from where we'd travelled, back from the single road through Denali.

I turned. The pavement was dark, no headlights. Maybe it was the wind.

No. The sound was louder now, a rumble.

I squinted and saw the flash of lights through the trees, just for a moment, then gone. The car was coming closer. I knew now that it was less than two hundred yards and closing. My legs turned to liquid. The sound bore down upon me. I held my breath.

The car screeched to a stop. It was completely dark, no headlights, no lights on inside. I took a cautious step toward it, then another.

"Tanya, no!" Connor called, his voice hoarse. They were the first words he'd spoken since we'd left the lodge.

The driver's side door opened.

"Tanya. It's okay, baby. It's me."

Cleo.

I melted. I'd been right. That voice was unmistakable.

"Are you . . ." I stammered. "What happened?"

"Can't talk now," she snapped. "Just get in the car."

I dragged Connor across the last stretch of pavement and threw open the back door.

Then I froze. There was someone else in the backseat, a man. I peered into the shadows. Maybe this was a trap. Maybe Rytech had recorded Cleo's voice to fool me. It would make sense, because at first I thought my eyes were playing tricks on me—

"Tanya," the man said.

That voice! He extended a hand. His fingers wrapped around my wrist. The feeling of his skin was so familiar.

"Dad?" I gasped.

"It's me. I'm all right." The words were a croak. He was weak.

But this was no trick. No technology could fool me once I saw the outline of his face. He pulled me into the car and wrapped his arms around me. I buried my face against his chest.

Chapter Twenty-One

Once we hit the highway, we drove in silence for what must have been an hour at least. No headlights passed us, racing in the opposite direction, back toward Denali. I decided to take that as a good sign. It meant that nobody from the outside was trying to cut off our escape—at least, not yet.

"How did you make it out?" I finally whispered to my father.

Dad chewed his lip, weighing his words. "You'll have to ask Cleo," he said, nodding toward the front seat. "She and Gretchen took a huge risk. And . . . Gretchen . . . she . . ."

"Gretchen knew the danger going in," Cleo finished. Her voice was low. "It's done."

They were silent after that. I didn't press them. Their fraught little exchange could only mean one thing: Gretchen was dead.

That sober reality jolted me. I no longer felt exhausted. Now I was frightened again. Gone was the dream-like reverie

I'd briefly enjoyed sitting beside my father. I let go of his hand. Questions began to race through my mind. I wanted to ask Cleo how she and Gretchen managed to get into that freakish prison, let alone free my dad from it. But I couldn't.

Instead I looked to Connor, slumped on the other side of the backseat, his head against the window. In the moonlight, I could see that his lips were cracked and dry.

"Connor's sick," I said. "He has a fever. We need to get him help as soon as possible."

Dad nodded absently. "He needs an antibiotic. It's the implant."

Without taking her eyes from the road, Cleo reached under the driver's seat and passed me a small plastic box, white with a red cross. "I've got the Makhorka tablets; give him a double dose."

My father watched wide-eyed as I opened the first aid kit: Band-Aids, Neosporin, tiny scissors . . . There was only one prescription bottle, unmarked. I twisted it and dumped two pills into my hand. Then I reached across Dad and shoved the pills in Connor's face.

Connor flinched.

"Take them," my father urged. He reached down and pulled the bottle of water from his feet. "You have to take them now or you'll die."

Before Connor could respond, I placed the pills in his mouth. Dad held the bottle to Connor's lips. As Connor swallowed, water spilled down his cheeks.

Dad handed the bottle to me.

"Watch," Cleo said, her eyes meeting mine in the rearview mirror. "He'll get better fast. It's like a miracle."

• • •

It wasn't long before the eastern horizon began to glow with a faint blue light. It was morning already. We'd traveled 145 miles, give or take. I was angry at myself for not knowing the distance exactly, but it was hard to concentrate. My dad kept shooting urgent glances toward Cleo in the front seat.

"I need to take a leak," Cleo suddenly announced. "Connor, what about you?"

He jerked up and shook his head. "I'm fine—"

"You should go," she interrupted. The car slowed to a stop, and she turned to lean across the driver's seat, meeting my dad's gaze. "You two stay here. Michael, honk if there's trouble."

Cleo took Connor's hand and led him into the brush on the side of the highway. I could see their frozen breath in the dawn light. Only when she glanced back did I realize this was as much for my father's benefit as for Connor's. Dad wanted a moment with me.

Yet once we were alone he said nothing.

Silence stretched between us.

"Dad?" I ventured.

"Cleo told me . . ." His voice cracked a little. "She told me all of it. How you crossed the entire country to find her. How dangerous it was for you. And how brave you were. How strong . . ." His hands trembled as he rested them over mine. He was trying hard not to cry. "Thank you, Tanya. Thank you for saving my life. I love you more than I'm even able to . . ." He tried to say more, but couldn't.

"It was just as much Cleo."

"Only because you found *her*. It's your gift—"

"It's not," I murmured, cutting him off. "I found her because I love you, too."

He blinked a few times and stared out the car window into the darkness, shaking his head.

"The people who did this to you . . . they're not all dead, are they?" I asked, clasping his fingers again. "More are still out there?"

Dad nodded uneasily, not turning toward me.

"How many more?"

He said nothing. His hands were shaking.

"Dad?"

"I don't really know." He took a deep breath and wiped his eyes.

"So what do we do?" I asked.

When he turned to me again, I saw it: that look, the one I'd grown up with, the one that told me he was puzzling over some problem that could be solved with just a little more concentration. I hadn't realized how much I missed that look until it was right in front of me, in the present.

He opened his mouth to answer, but Cleo and Connor had returned.

"We need gas," Cleo said around midday. We'd passed very few rest stops, but now in the distance I could see an old-time gas station and convenience mart. "Tanya, I'll need you to get water, a fever reducer for Connor, and some food. We have a long drive."

She handed me a credit card. Gold, Visa. The cardholder's name was Sarah M. Smith.

I didn't protest.

Inside the roadside gas station shop, the rows of brightly colored candy packages and potato chips looked surreal to me. Last night, I'd been certain that Connor and I would die in the wilderness; now I was trolling the aisles of a convenience store. I tried to focus. *Get what you need and get out. Water, fever reducer, food.*

A Slurpee machine churned Day-Glo orange and blue drinks near the cash register. I took the bottles of water, aspirin, and a couple bags of nuts and chips to the counter to pay. The man behind the counter had his back to me, his eyes glued to a small TV with wire rigged up the wall.

"Hey," I said loudly to get the man's attention. Slowly, he turned around, still keeping one eye on the TV.

"That be all?" He chewed tobacco and spat some out in a Slurpee cup.

"And the gas," I handed him the credit card.

It was some news network, a fuzzy aerial shot of a huge fire—flames and dark smoke filling the sky. Below in bright red and all caps: *BREAKING NEWS: EXPLOSION AT DENALI NATIONAL PARK.*

I stared at screen, unable to comprehend what exactly I was seeing. The clerk picked up a remote and pumped up the volume.

"A subterranean explosion at Denali National Park has sparked major wild fires," the newscaster reported. "No one can confirm what caused the blast, but as of now the consensus among geologists and other experts is that a dormant underground volcano erupted . . ."

"Just need your autograph," the clerk said.

He handed me the receipt to sign.

I stepped back, unable to speak. What had Cleo and Gretchen done? I felt dizzy. I signed in a scribble, grabbed the bag on the counter, and hurried out the door.

I still couldn't speak when I got in the car.

Instead of getting in the back again, I sat in the front passenger seat.

Once we were back on the highway I turned to Cleo.

"I saw the news in the gas station. There was an explosion at Denali."

Cleo sniffed. "Really? You don't say?"

"What did you do?"

"We did what we had to. For all of us to make it." Cleo gripped the wheel tightly, her eyes flashing to the rear-view mirror. "*All* of us." She shot me a dirty look, and then smirked. "When will you learn not to ask so many questions?"

"All of you?" my father gasped from the backseat. "Gretchen, too?"

"How do you think I got the car, Michael? Gretchen's got more lives than a cat." Cleo shot me another cold glare.

I nodded, knowing not to ask anything more.

"Next time we stop, I think I'll get in the backseat now and take a nap," I said to her. I turned and looked at Connor, slumped against my father, snoring.

Dad was shaking his head with an expression of joy and bewilderment.

"Miracle after miracle," he breathed.

Without warning, he reached for my hand and gripped it,

harder than he had before. I gripped back, savouring the fact
that he was alive. Again, his calloused fingers felt so familiar,
but alien, too. And in that moment, I understood how he felt
. . . not about me, but about Gretchen.

It would take time for him to adjust. Not as long as it
would take me, but still. After all, Gretchen had been dead
for only a few hours before being resurrected. For me, Dad
had been dead for over a year.

I must have relaxed at some point because I fell asleep. When
I woke up it was morning. Cleo was asleep in the front passenger seat; my dad was driving. The road was bumpy.

Connor was sleeping beside me. I touched his forehead.
It was warm but not hot. I didn't expect to feel the relief so
strongly, but tears streamed down my face. Cleo hadn't lied.
Connor would be all right.

It wasn't quite 7 A.M., but through the windows I could
tell that the sun was already blistering in the sky. I squinted
out the window. We were on a back road in some sort of
desert wasteland, an unforgiving cactus patch. Several large
aluminum signs passed as we bounced along.

AMWAY LOGGING.
NO TRESPASSING.
ALL TRESPASSERS WILL BE PROSECUTED.
ACTIVE LOGGING: DANGER KEEP OUT.

I noticed two surveillance cameras protruding from the
limbs of a small cactus plant.

Connor stiffened beside me.

"It's all right," I said.

My voice was hoarse; I hadn't spoken in hours. We were in survival mode now. A diet of truck stop snacks. Napping in turns. Even then, barely sleeping. All along: knowing the odds were too high that whatever had been implanted in Connor's and Dad's chests were tracking their every move.

We'd silently clung to the hope that the chaos Cleo and Gretchen had left in their wake had bought us a head-start to wherever we were going, that whatever signal Connor and Dad were emitting would no longer be detectable. But that's all it was: hope.

The road crested upward.

I touched Connor's arm as Dad jerked to a stop at the top of the ridge.

The windows rolled down. In the silence, the four of us exited the car. We slammed the doors. I could hear the sound of dogs barking and chickens squawking.

Together we stared down at a familiar clump of rustic bungalows and a community garden. A mosquito buzzed around our heads. I swatted it away. Connor swayed slightly on his feet. I steadied him and sucked in a breath: *Cleo's home.* There it was: perched at the end of the cul-de-sac, the white stucco and red slate roof. I could see the main road snaking off toward the highway, lost in the hazy horizon.

I started down the path, with Connor and my dad and Cleo a few paces behind . . . until I couldn't help myself. I broke into a run on the jagged stones to Cleo's front door, glancing back to make sure the three were right behind me.

"You don't know how happy I am to be here," Dad gasped. "I never thought I'd see this place again."

Cleo laughed, not winded in the least. She slapped my father's back. "Me neither." She whistled to her dogs. "Here, boys!"

As they bounded toward us excitedly, I saw a man in a raggedy T-shirt and jeans with long hair and a beard standing in the distance, pointing a hunting rifle at us. Cleo followed my gaze and froze.

"Bill, it's me!" she yelled.

He lowered the rifle, lifting up his sunglasses, peering at us.

"You okay? What's with the company?"

"Friends."

"Friends? Where you been Cleo?"

"Long story, Bill." Cleo kneeled to the ground, hugging her dogs. "Hey guys, I missed you. I hope Bill took good care of you." She turned and ran up the path to her front door and its rusted, decades-old mailbox.

I watched as she touched her thumb to a screen hidden beneath it. The screen flashed green and the door opened.

Chapter Twenty-Two

"I didn't know what to think," Bill muttered. He was repeating himself. Everybody seemed to be talking at once, not that I could blame them, except Connor and me. We'd gathered in Cleo's cramped living room, I sat mushed between my father and Connor. I hadn't let go of my father's hand. We watched Bill pacing back and forth like a cat.

"You never miss our weekly check-ins," he added. "Not once in . . . how many years now? Twelve?"

"Something like that," Cleo answered.

"I knew something had to be wrong, so I got here as fast as I—"

"I'm sorry," Dad interrupted, eyeing Bill warily. "But you are with Cleo?"

"Relax, Michael," she said, gently. "Bill's an old and dear friend, like you. In fact, he was the one who trained me, helped me set myself up here, where we can't be found. Bill used to work . . . where I once worked. In a former life."

Bill registered no response. That part of the conversation was over. "Where's Gretchen?" he asked. "I tried her too, figuring she'd be with you."

"She was," Cleo said. She turned to the window. Her jaw twitched. "She's gone."

"Gone?" I asked. "You mean—?"

"Yes." Cleo gave a grim nod and stepped toward the dusty glass pane, peering upward toward the sky, maybe searching for any potential danger. A shaft of sunlight illuminated her face. "I'm not allowing myself to fully process it. Not until I'm sure your dad and Connor are safe. That's what Gretchen gave her life for, and you better believe that's what I'm gonna see through." She turned back to us. "There'll be plenty of time for tears later."

I stared at her, wanting to know

"Honey, I don't have time to fill in the blanks," Cleo continued, reading my thoughts. "I'll walk you through the whole brutal ordeal later if you want me to." She shared a brief, meaningful look with Dad. "But first things first. Whatever it is that Rytech implanted in Michael and Connor needs to come out. This place is secure enough for now, but it's far from fail-safe. My jammers can only scramble frequencies for so long." She turned to Bill. "You've dug bullets out before, right?"

Bill nodded and shrugged. "Just a few, yeah."

"And you've got surgical equipment next door?"

He was already on the move, grabbing the shotgun he'd leaned against the doorjamb. "I'll bring over whatever I've got. I'm sure we can make do."

"Thanks, Bill."

"Sure thing." He ducked out the door.

Cleo then turned to Connor. She hesitated, perhaps only now realizing how pale he looked. "Connor? You okay?"

"More or less," he said, trying to sound brave.

"You must be hungry."

"I was before. Not so much now."

Cleo returned a sympathetic smile. "This'll be over soon enough. In the meantime, let's get you some air."

I looked to my father for a word of reassurance as to when we could expect Connor to feel better. But he was staring into space with a strange, haunted intensity.

"We can pick some veggies from my garden, see what I can whip up for us," Cleo added, glancing at Dad. She paused. "Michael, what's—"

"Do you have an untraceable landline?" Dad asked urgently.

"Of course. Why? What do you have in mind?"

He hopped to his feet. "Trust me."

Cleo's speakerphone rustled with the sound of someone picking up on the other end. A moment's silence followed. I held my breath as Harrison's voice echoed in Cleo's living room.

"Hello?"

Harrison sounded guarded. Wary. And too haggard to disguise anxiety. "Hello? Who is this?"

"It's me," my father said softly.

There was a sharp breath. "Michael? How . . . ?" His question trailed off as soon as it began.

"How'd I survive Alaska?" Despite Dad's effort to sound

calm, I heard an anger that chilled me. He spoke as if he were alone in the room, even though Connor, Cleo, and I were all staring at him. "Doesn't matter. All that matters is that I did. As did my daughter." He allowed Harrison a moment to process this information. "I will never forgive you for going after Tanya. But you already know that. I get why you sold me out. You are who you are. I should have known as much. But my—"

"Michael, you don't understand," Harrison interrupted. "I made a mistake, yes, but I tried to stop them once I realized how far—"

"Save it, Harrison. I didn't call for a reckoning, or even an apology."

More rustling. "Then why did you call?"

"Because I thought you might want to speak with your son."

I held my breath again. Once more there was dead silence. "Connor's . . . with you?" Harrison asked. His voice was hoarse.

"He is."

Harrison breathed harder, then sniffed. Was he crying? I didn't care; he deserved to feel pain. My eyes darted to Connor. He'd stood and begun to pace, as Bill had before, his sickly skin damp once more with perspiration. Where *was* Bill? Shouldn't he have returned by now? For his *own* safety? Bill understood the urgency. Weren't he and Cleo confident that he had whatever he needed to dig the toxic metal out of Connor and my father?

"I—I have to speak to him," Harrison stammered. "Please, Michael . . ."

My father glanced over at Connor, who'd stopped two feet to Dad's right. Connor's expression hardened. He gazed at the speakerphone, his fists balled tightly at his sides. He nodded.

"That depends," my father said.

"Depends on what?" Harrison asked.

"On what you're prepared to do."

"You're . . . You're blackmailing me?"

Dad said nothing. And then Harrison did the strangest thing: he laughed. There was no joy in it, of course. Only irony. "You know, he's the only reason I didn't blow the whistle on all of this. Because I knew his life was in their hands. They were using Connor to make sure I stayed silent. And now I'm guessing you're going to use him to make sure I don't."

Again, Dad said nothing.

"Let me hear his voice, and I give you my word—"

"Your word," Dad repeated hollowly.

Connor's lips twisted in a scowl. He glanced at me and shook his head.

"I swear to you, Michael, I will make this right," Harrison pleaded.

"Meaning you'll turn yourself in to the authorities and admit to everything."

"Michael, don't be naïve," Harrison said. For the first time, there was a cryptic note of defeat in his voice.

"About what?" Dad spat.

"About *Rytech*," Harrison snapped back. "I'd be dead long before I could reach any kind of 'authority' who might care." He lingered on the word "authority," driving home either pity or disdain or both. "If this phone conversation lasts any longer, I very well might be dead before I hang up—"

"I hate you," Connor said, cutting off his father in mid-sentence.

"Connor? Son?"

Harrison sounded so scared now. Scared of losing his only child. Scared because he knew he already had. Dad raised his face from the speakerphone to find Cleo staring back at him, equally unnerved. For the first time, I saw something resembling fear in her eyes, too. We were all terrified. And for what? Who stood to gain, in the end? Who *was* Rytech, anyway?

"Connor?" the disembodied voice asked. "Are you there?"

"Fix this," Connor replied. His words were strangled. "Find a way to fix this. Or you will never see or hear from me again."

"I will, Con," Harrison promised urgently. "I swear to you, I will. Just don't give up on . . ." His voice trailed off. There was a screech—maybe a chair scraping on a metal floor—and Harrison's voice blared into the speaker, distorted. "No, wait—"

Pop. Something silenced him. It wasn't terribly loud, but it was followed a moment later by the dull thud of a fall.

My heart squeezed; I looked to Cleo, who shut her eyes, stricken. Dad spun to Connor and reached for him, but Connor was already starting to tremble.

"Who is this?" a woman's voice asked

I gaped at the speaker in horror. I recognized the voice immediately: Alison from Rytech.

Cleo abruptly dove for the speakerphone and hung up.

She didn't need to explain. The expression she'd been wearing from the moment Connor spoke up said it all. We were in more danger than we thought. Only then did another fear enter my mind—one that had been hovering just outside the place where, until now, my imagination refused to go. But this proved that there was no place too dark, too unfathomable.

"What about Beth?" I asked Dad and Cleo.

Chapter Twenty-Three

Cleo stood in front of her laptop, typing furiously.

Dad was now the one pacing—right behind her, unable to conceal his anxiety. "It's seven-thirty A.M. here," he muttered, "which means it's nine-thirty back home."

"Which means she'll be at school," I reassured him.

It struck me as odd that I'd come up with the plan. Especially since I'd done it in about thirty seconds; not to mention the fact that I was sleep-deprived, terrified, hungry, thirsty, a *teenager*—and Cleo was a professional who trafficked for a living in these sorts of nightmare scenarios. On the other hand, I knew Beth better than anyone here. At this point in our lives, that included Dad, too. We both knew it without having to discuss it.

During the summer, the elementary school where Beth taught was converted into a sort of makeshift "arts camp" for kids aged 3-12. It was really just glorified day care. Beth's skills as a kindergarten teacher made her the ideal arts and crafts counselor for the youngest campers. Mostly, it was a way to keep her busy and occupied, to keep her mind off of the cold reality that she was a childless widow, shackled with an ungrateful stepdaughter.

Cleo glanced up from her laptop, her fingers still tapping. "Does Beth have a desktop or a laptop?"

"Desktop," I said.

"Hmm," Cleo mused, her eyes pinging back to her laptop screen, with its lines of code streaming down as fast as falling rain. "That means it's on the school's server, which'll probably only have a few firewalls to breach. Hopefully nothing too exotic . . ." She continued clacking away on her keyboard, and then looked up. "Okay, I'm in."

She tilted her laptop so we could all see her screen. On it was a window showing what looked at first like a video feed.

All at once I realized it was the camera on Beth's desktop computer.

We were looking into her classroom, where a group of small children were finger painting. Beth crossed before the camera lens, crouching at the table. She was wearing a sundress I recognized. My throat caught. It was so strange that the dress had always annoyed me; its preppy blue pattern seemed to distill the person I once thought Beth was: the pretty gold digger. Now I wished I could dive through the screen and hug her in that dress, shield her. Nothing in Beth's face or body language suggested she knew she was in any danger.

Dad managed to exhale.

"Okay." Cleo nodded to me. "Call her."

I started dialing Beth's cell phone number on Cleo's

landline. We were all silent for a moment. I prayed that the line was still untraceable.

"Remember," Cleo warned me, "keep it brief. My phone's software will scramble the audio on our end in case someone is eavesdropping, and we should assume someone will be. But Beth will be loud and clear to whoever's listening in."

I nodded. My heart pounded loudly in my chest.

The phone began to ring.

I watched as Beth stepped away from the table, frowning at her pocket. She pulled out the phone and stared at it, and then brought it to her ear.

"Hello?"

There was a tiny delay between her response and the sound of her voice.

"Beth, it's me," I blurted out. "I'm safe, I swear, but please, whatever you do, don't say my name, okay?"

Her voice quaking, Beth managed to utter: "I . . . I don't . . . Oh thank God."

"I'm fine," I assured her. "But I need you to listen to me right now and try not to talk any more than you absolutely have to."

She moved toward her desk, filling the screen. "I don't understand—"

"I know you don't," I cut in. "But it's really important that you try to sound as casual and as normal as you can right now. I'm going to tell you something, then give you instructions." I took a breath, realizing how hard it was going to be for her to do what I'd just asked. "Dad is alive."

On Cleo's laptop, I saw Beth grab hold of a corner of the desk to steady herself. Fearing that she might actually faint,

I turned to Dad; he must've been thinking the same thing, because when he leaned closer to the phone's speaker, he spoke as gently as I'd ever heard him.

"Hello, Beth."

We stared as Beth froze. Her face was turned away from us, but I could hear her trying her best not to break down completely in the middle of a roomful of finger-painting children. "I . . . I . . ."

"Shh," Dad soothed. "It's all right. I'll explain it all to you very soon, I promise. I love you so much." He looked over at me, then added, "We both do."

"Please," Beth pleaded in a strained voice. "I don't understand—"

"I know you don't, sweetheart," Dad continued. "But you will."

Cleo cleared her throat, reminding us that time was of the essence. I couldn't wait for Dad to compose himself. "Beth, we need your help," I stated. "Right now."

"But . . ." Her voice fell to a whisper. "I'm standing in a classroom full of five-year-olds."

"I know," I said. "We're watching you from your computer."

"What? How . . . ?" She started to turn, and I realized there was really no point in my having told her that.

"Please, Beth, don't worry about it," I urged. "You just need to focus on what I'm saying to you, because I need to hang up soon."

"Okay," Beth said, trying to sound calm. "How can I help you, miss?"

I almost rolled my eyes at her clumsy attempt at subterfuge.

But she was holding it together. I had to give her credit for even trying. All at once I felt a flash of rage—maybe something akin to what Connor had felt toward his father, was probably still feeling, even now—rage at Rytech for putting Beth in this position. She was a teacher. Of *toddlers*. A person with a good heart . . . a heart that did not deserve to be manipulated or poisoned with an implant or watched from a satellite. And now she could very well end up like Harrison, too: a lifeless body collapsing to a floor somewhere, felled by Rytech under their all-seeing gaze.

Cleo jabbed a finger at her wrist, tapping an invisible wristwatch.

"We're going to send you a link to a file," I said in a rush. "Nothing complicated, just a document Dad's writing up, explaining everything that's happened, and who to forward the information to. Give us a few more minutes, then look in your junk folder."

"But how . . ." Beth stopped herself, remembering to keep her language cryptic. "How will I recognize this . . . package?"

"Don't worry," I said. "You will. What's important is that you open it right away, and immediately follow the instructions in the document. Okay?"

"Okay." Beth chewed her lip and glanced back toward her computer. As much as it pained me to do so, I hung up.

The screen went black. She was gone.

I felt Dad's hand on my shoulder. I squeezed it, blinking away tears as I turned and watched him hand a cell phone to Cleo.

"This has everything," he said gravely. "Everything *I* know about Rytech, anyway."

Cleo took the phone and shoved the metallic end of a

white plastic cube into the charger port. The cube glowed blue for an instant; she removed it and triggered a hidden lid on the other side, popping it open to reveal a USB—which she promptly stuck into the laptop. Once again, the screen became a cascade of unfathomable code.

"I'm in Beth's spam folder now," Cleo said. "Uploading."

In a flash the screen shifted to a normal-looking mailbox. There was a new unread email in the folder. Dad squeezed my shoulder again as we silently read the code words I'd come up with: *Your purchase of The End of the Affair by Graham Greene has shipped.* It was the first idea that had popped into my head, but Dad knew it was a clue she was sure to recognize.

Cleo closed the laptop and sighed. I exchanged a quick smile with Dad, until we were interrupted by a groan from Connor. We regarded him anxiously. He was sprawled on the couch, his face a chalky white. Beads of sweat glistened on his neck; his T-shirt was damp. His chest seemed to shudder with each breath.

"When Bill gets here for the home surgery, Connor goes first," Dad muttered. He moved to the window and squinted outside. "He's been gone a little while now. Wonder what's taking him?"

Cleo frowned. "Yeah, I—" She broke off and stiffened, raising a finger to her lips.

My heart thumped. Whatever she was listening for, I heard it now, too: a low and steady whirring. Rhythmic, getting closer—

"Helicopters." Dad gasped, backing away from the windowpane. "How'd they find us?"

But he knew the answer, as did I. It's strange, how some-times a puzzle piece you've been holding in your hand can suddenly seem like such an obvious fit. I quickly turned to Cleo. "Bill . . . ?"

The ashen look on her face confirmed that she was cycling through the same fears that I was. Maybe Bill wasn't as trust-worthy as she'd assumed. Or maybe he no longer trusted *her*. He'd been ready to shoot Connor and me when we'd first arrived; he'd been suspicious of Dad, too. He mentioned to Cleo that she'd broken off their usual contact. Maybe he thought *she'd* been corrupted. Or maybe he simply knew what our whereabouts would be worth, and was going for a huge payday. The reason didn't matter, though.

"Look out," Connor suddenly hissed. Before I could even process what was happening, he'd leaped off the couch and charged at me. In the corner of my eye I glimpsed Bill standing outside the window where Dad had been standing seconds ago, shotgun raised. I felt the impact of Connor tackling me just as I heard the gunshot go off, glass exploding everywhere as the window shattered. Then I was on the ground, wincing, Connor nearly smothered me in the hopes of shielding my body with his own. I managed to look up; Bill was already gone, a cloud of dust in his place. The roar of the helicopter rotors was deafening now.

Behind me I could hear the pounding of feet as Cleo and my dad raced into the next room. "How many helicopters?" I heard Dad shout over the noise.

"I count two!" Cleo shouted back, and then I heard her inhale sharply. "My guns!" Drawers and cabinets opened and slammed shut. "They're gone. Bill must have cleaned me out before I got home." Cleo's voice rose; for the first time, she sounded panicked. "This was all a trap . . . Michael, I'm so sorry—"

"You must have *something* we can use," Dad shouted, his frantic voice all but swallowed by the helicopter noise.

The floor shook. They were directly above us. We had to get out. I elbowed Connor, who rolled off me with a moan, and I helped him to his feet. Dad hurried toward us, Cleo trailing close behind him, carrying what looked like an over-sized toy pistol.

"All I could find was an old flare gun and a couple of flares," she yelled.

Dad's eyes met mine. For a moment I felt as if someone had hit the pause button on the world. We stared at each other in this strangely frozen stretch of time, searching each other's faces, silently asking in unison: *Am I prepared to do this?*

The world snapped back into motion.

"What's the range of the flare gun?" I shouted at Cleo.

Cleo's face twisted; she was baffled. I couldn't blame her. It was as if I'd asked her what color her drapes were while her house was burning down. But after a quick glance at my father, who nodded in return, she shrugged. There was nothing left to lose at this point.

"Maximum a thousand feet. Then the flare detonates like a firework."

"Do you think the helicopters will come that close?" I asked.

"They already are!" The veins in her neck bulged; Cleo had to scream now to make herself heard, driving home the point. She ducked her head out of the broken window, then just as quickly withdrew. "They're Comanches. They can fly as low as they want."

Dad gazed at me, jerking his head toward the window.

My legs felt numb as I forced myself to Cleo's side. The hot wind and dust stung my eyes.

"Don't fire until I say so," I said. I crouched low on the shards of broken glass to get a better view up toward the sky. There they were: two black hovering shapes, like giant insects against a cloudless blue void. I swallowed hard, my heart beating in my chest, and stared. This was the only true gift I'd ever had, intuiting distances with only my gut to go on: "The closer one is 1,100 feet away," I announced. "It's descending . . . 1,050 . . . 1,020 . . ." The sun formed a blinding halo behind the rotor. I had to shield my eyes, squinting against the glare. "1,010 . . . 1,000 feet . . . 995 feet . . . Okay, Cleo—*now*."

Cleo squeezed the trigger. The force jerked her back against me. A bright pink light rocketed up from the window, whistling as it arced straight toward the helicopter. Once again, time seemed to stop. I saw it shatter the glass of the cockpit. And then it exploded.

My jaw dropped.

I gazed, awestruck, as pieces of helicopter debris fell. It reminded me of candy from a punctured piñata. The bulk of the aircraft began to pinwheel wildly. Seconds later it careened into the second helicopter. The sunlight was too much; I squeezed my eyes shut. There was a terrible metal screeching sound. It ended in a thunderous explosion over the hill from where we'd first arrived.

I opened my eyes. Thick plumes of black smoke rose from just beyond the barren horizon.

None of us said a word.

Cleo's whisper finally broke the eerie stillness.

"Beth opened the file," she said. Turning to look, I found her standing before her laptop, now open again. A shaky smile formed on her lips. "If she followed the instructions, that file's been forwarded to the inboxes of the biggest media outlets in the country."

I looked to Connor, then to my dad.

"You did it, Tanya," Dad said softly.

Connor nodded, and took my hand in his, squeezing it tight.

"Let's get out of here," I said.

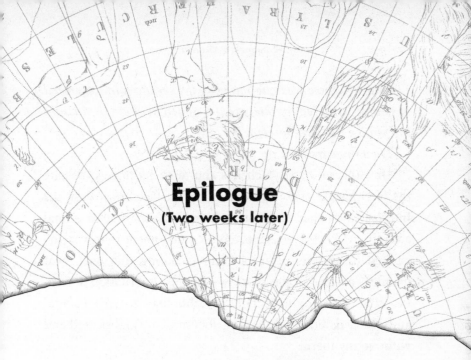

Epilogue
(Two weeks later)

Logan International is too risky, so we take a commuter flight from Hartford to Chicago O'Hare. I glance down at the small sheath of stapled tickets in my hand. Flight 829 to London Heathrow is scheduled to begin boarding in just a few minutes. London to Dubai, Dubai to Lagos, Lagos to Madagascar.

Madagascar had been Connor's idea, of course. The one place in the world he'd always wanted to visit.

I lift my head and peer around the terminal, anxious for Connor to return from the snack bar. I know he has to eat or drink; his body is still weak. But I still don't like being apart from him for even a small length of time. My gaze sweeps my surroundings, and lands on one of the terminal's plasma screens on which CNN is playing. An anchorwoman I don't recognize is concluding a report on an outbreak of E.coli at five fast food restaurants in the Pacific Northwest. Three deaths have been reported so far.

I start to look away, wondering if I should join the crowd of people gathered by the gate. I want to be there the instant they make the announcement.

Then my ears perk up.

"In other news, Rytech has shuttered its offices, despite the fact that no new information has surfaced regarding the Internet hoax that implicated the tech company in a global conspiracy. Earlier we reported on a document that was circulated to various news outlets—including this one—that detailed an elaborate plot by various international entities that used sophisticated biotechnology to spy. Federal authorities determined that the document was fabricated and without any merit.

"In a related story, no definitive cause has been attributed to the mysterious explosion in Alaska's Denali National Park, also referenced in the phony document.

"That's it for national news, and now moving on to entertainment. A handful of new films are opening at the box office this weekend . . ."

I tune her out and sigh to myself. What else can I do? Like Dad said, we did our best, but our best was only good enough to save ourselves. The people who were ultimately behind Rytech's sinister research will probably stay hidden, at least for now. But I know one thing: they're going to have a much harder time finishing what they started now. Hoaxes have been proven real in the past.

Haven't they?

"Ladies and gentlemen," *a pleasant-sounding man announces over the loudspeaker,* "We'd like to invite our First Class cabin to begin boarding at this time . . ."

I feel a knot tighten in my stomach, and turn to see Connor smiling down at me apologetically, a pair of granola bars in one hand. As always, I marvel at how he looks like himself again—the boy I'd always prayed would come back to me—in spite of what's still buried inside his chest. I was so sure he wouldn't make it.

"I didn't know which kind you'd want, so I can just eat whichever one you don't," he says.

"Thanks." I reach for the dark chocolate but instead take his free hand.

My fingers clasp his, lingering for a moment.

He gently squeezes back. "We should board. Are you ready, Reese?"

I smile at the alias in spite of myself. But then I'm all business, tucking my plane tickets into the passport Cleo forged for me. She fabricated a phony identity for Connor as well. As I secure my tickets between the passport's stiff pages, I glimpse the recent photo laminated beside my name: Reese Perry.

Together we join the crush of people anxious to board.

It's an eight-hour flight to London. Outside the terminal, beyond the floor-to-ceiling windows, the Midwestern sun is pale and bright. In my mind's eye, I see our flight path in a graceful arc above the curve of the earth, 3,958 miles over land and ocean.

We've almost reached the gate attendant when I feel my phone vibrating in my jeans pocket. I pause and fish it out.

There's a text from Graham Greene.

I click on the image. It's a selfie of Dad and Beth, standing on a beach, their tanned arms wrapped around *each other, their smiling faces sun-kissed. They look tired. But I see in my dad's eyes what I'd lost and hoped to find. I see it in Beth's eyes, too.*

See u both soon, *I text him back.*

Acknowledgments

We are deeply grateful to our smart, funny, and incredible editor, Dan Ehrenhaft, without whom this book would never even exist. We'd also like to thank the whole team at Soho Press, especially Rachel Kowal, Janine Agro, Meredith Barnes, Amara Hoshijo, and most of all, publisher Bronwen Hruska.